Armageddon

Daniel Fulton

Pi-Writers Press

Contents

1

Dark Times

E lezar Aronivich stood at the side of the wood-en, government-Issue coffin where his father lay. He had a few minutes alone with him before he would be taken to the ovens to be cremated. No one had a choice now. The death rate from all the war, famine, and disease mandated the practice. Mounds of ash were buried outside the city of Jerusalem daily.

Elezar took out the knife he carried at all times and cut off his Parot, the lock of hair every Haredi Jew wore from his sideburns to announce to the world his religion and placed it in his father's cold hands. Elezar practiced the rote religious rituals of his Father out of respect.

Now that the last of Elezar's immediate family was lying dead before him, he no longer felt the need to keep up the charade. It all felt so confining, and empty. If there was a God, Elezar was sure he wasn't a Haredi.

"Move along," the soldier prodded with the end of his gun. Elezar complied immediately. He didn't think his scull could take another blow from the butt of a weapon.

He took off his top hat and removed his full-length trench coat, trappings of the faith he no longer followed, tossed them aside, and ran away while the guard was busy preparing the body for the fire. He didn't need a God. He would survive on his own!

I can't go home, he thought. The firefight destroyed it, and besides, they might come looking for me.

Even though he didn't believe in God, he still wouldn't get the mark of the Beast. Religion had nothing to do with it; He didn't trust the government and their techno-tracking goons. He didn't need the worthless bitcoin they gave out. He knew many who were surviving on the fringes of society using the barter system who hated the Beast for the tyrant he was.

He did have an estranged uncle on his mother's side of the family. He had only seen him at his mother's funeral. He came into the viewing after Elezar's father left to pay his respects.

He was banished from the family for converting to Christianity. His name was Benjamin Ben-Hadid, and he owned a bakery company that made most of the bread consumed in the city. For that reason, he was spared most of the persecution Christians and Jews faced.

He refused the Mark also so he couldn't directly purchase his raw materials, but there were always workers of the Realm eager to do the marketing and purchasing. They made it very lucrative for themselves. Maybe he could get a job under the table working for his uncle.

"I need a place to crash," Elezar said out loud.

He walked around near his old neighborhood scouting places. The sun was casting ominous shadows on the street when he settled on a deserted upper story flat that had a window to the street and a stairway easily hidden by the night. He settled in just before the darkness brought out the highwaymen and the murderers that lurked in the shadows. They preyed on anyone they perceived as weak and defenseless.

He dozed off occasionally only to wake with a start, remembering the last image he had of his father. The last time he saw his father alive, Elezar was clinging to him, pulling against the troopers, trying to free him until a gun butt to the back of Elezar's skull ended his struggle.

They fled into the street after the tear gas and before the percussion bomb. The troopers got a perverse pleasure from the devastation caused by the bomb and used them indiscriminately, even after the people had surrendered, just to see the carnage.

Maybe if he had held on tighter, pulled harder, and fought better, his father would be alive today. The grief and guilt caused him to tremble. His eyes refused to close; his mind ravaged with the image.

The sun chased away the shadows too soon. His stiff body groaned, and his head spun when he finally had the courage to get up. He staggered unsteadily and leaned against the wall to steady himself against the spinning room. He touched the bruise on the back of his head gingerly and waited to move until the room stopped spinning. He was hurt worse than he would admit but going to the doctor required the mark.

He stumbled down the stairs hanging on to both banisters for safety. He turned into the street. The sun was in its full morning glory and his eyes couldn't seem to adjust. He stopped, leaned against the wall and opened his eyes slowly. When he could make out the silhouette of the sidewalk he staggered off, never too far from a wall or a lamppost.

His youthful twenty-one years meant the odds of getting over his head injury quickly were in his favor, but the weight of his survivor's guilt was a heavy burden.

It seemed the longer he walked the steadier he became. His mind and his muscles had come to some sort of compromise allowing him more balance and movement. His belly finally burrowed its warning through his grief. He hadn't eaten much two days before and nothing yesterday. Another day without a morsel of food and some potable water might bring him down in his weakened state.

"I've got to find something to eat," he lamented under his breath, with his hand on his stomach.

He made his way to his uncle's bread factory hoping that his father's rigid beliefs and bigoted behavior would not be cast upon him!

The mid-morning sun baked his shoulders and pierced his eyes.

He thought about stopping to rest but was afraid he might not be strong enough to get back up. The closer he got to his destination, the stronger the aroma of the bakery became. His stomach howled in anger, forcing him to press on.

The service entrance vibrated with the heavy trucks as they brought more grain, sugar, and all the things his uncle needed to produce the Beast's favorite bread. His bakery got top priority even in these times of famine because of the Beast's preference.

Elezar noticed the trucks stopped momentarily at the gate to show the guard a permit and bill of lading papers. Although he was supposed to get out of his shack and physically inspect the trucks, the gate keeper looked briefly at the papers and waved the trucks on.

The gate keeper seemed to think it was all such a bother when the trucks disturbed his nap. The amygdaloideum laced water that all the servants of the Realm were addicted to sapped any ambition or work ethic out of them; this guard included. Elezar was glad that he was one of the lucky ones not affected by the misery in a bottle. For some reason that he or anyone else could explain, Jews were the least likely to be addicted to it.

Elezar would take advantage of the guard's complacency. He walked further up the street, unnoticed by the guard in the shack, and waited out of sight for the next truck. The truck stopped at the gate and the "driver" thrust his papers out the window for the keeper of the gate to see.

The guy in the truck didn't know how to drive a truck. No drivers were needed. He was there to thwart any attempted hijackings. He was never more than a panic button away from drone air patrols that gave any potential hijackers an all-expenses paid trip to the ash dump outside the city.

Elezar ran to the truck on the right side and hunched over at the back wheels. When the truck started to move past the gate, he moved with it as it positioned itself to back into the dock to be unloaded. The truck gently nudged the dock. The airbrakes hissed as Elezar made his way up the steps.

When he reached the back of the truck, he tugged open the overhead sliding door of the truck like he was the driver. The dock foreman strolled over and asked for the papers.

"I'm just a trainee. The man in charge will be here shortly," said Elezar.

He stepped back from the door just as the driver reached the back of the truck with the papers. While the foreman and the driver were distracted, Elezar disappeared behind the skids full of sacks of flour. He made his way between the wall and the skids, stopping to peek around the corner at every isle way, and then hurried past to the next group of skids.

He finally saw a metal stairway leading to the main floor of the factory. A man was entering the stairs with one sack of flour slung over his shoulder. The placard over the door said QUALITY CONTROL so Elezar grabbed a sack of a slightly different color from a different skid and hurried to catch the man entering the stairway.

He heard the buzz of the electronic lock and saw the door swing open wide and the man enter into a hallway and turn right. Elezar used what strength he had left to bound up the stairs to catch the closing door with his outstretched fingers, just before it latched. He swung it open again and entered the hallway and went left. He was breathing hard from the exertion, so he ducked into an empty conference room and ditched the flour sack. He leaned against a long table physically exhausted.

He turned and looked out the window for some clue how to get to his uncle. He exited back into the hall and noticed the office roster on the wall at the other end of the hall. He walked down the hall like he was supposed to be there. Thankfully, he didn't meet anyone on the way. He found

Benjamin Ben-Hadid's name on the third floor. No number, just the entire third floor. An elevator to his left whisked him away. He was glad he didn't have to climb any more stairs. The third-floor doors opened.

A huge door opened into a suite of offices, the largest in the middle flanked by smaller ones on either side. Three desks sat obstructing the direct path into each office but only the middle one was occupied. It all spoke of a different time when the company flourished under a different system, a freer system, without all the layers of paperwork and mandated government employees there to tell the bread maker how to make bread.

The receptionist (spy?) diverted her eyes from her magazine and confronted Elezar. She noticed right away he didn't have the mark and he wasn't dressed in the proper company attire.

"How did you get in here?!" she exclaimed. "This is off limits to the public!"

She had her finger on the security button ready to call in the goons.

"Benjamin is my uncle!" Elezar exclaimed loudly, hoping to get his uncle's attention through the door.

She pushed the button and reached for her weapon.

Benjamin heard the commotion and came out of his office. He stopped in his tracks. Although he'd only seen Elezar once, at his sister's funeral, he knew him instantly. He rushed to embrace him.

"Elezar! I see my sister in your eyes and in your face! How are you? You look so thin! What have you been doing with yourself?"

Benjamin's questions came rapid fire, and then his voice changed.

"How is your father?" he said in a subdued voice.

"He died in a raid three days ago and they came for him yesterday." Elezar stammered.

"I'm so sorry, He was a good man."

"How can you say that after what he did to you?" Elezar anguished.

"Yes, he was a rigid, legalistic fanatic, but he was doing what his principles mandated. I didn't agree with his methods or his ideology, but I admire his conviction and he loved you and my sister dearly.

Elezar didn't answer his uncle's question. He was deep in thought pondering what his uncle said, grateful for his attitude.

Ben knew Elezar was not there for a social visit.

"Wanda, would you go to the Quality Control lab and get the latest data, they haven't sent a thing today. I need to know if their computers are down again. I'll be OK here with Elezar until you return." Ben asked.

She nodded and left the room.

"I need a job Uncle!" Elezar blurted as soon as she was gone, "I have nothing and nobody to turn to but you. Since I refuse the mark, I can't get a job in the Realm."

"I couldn't pay you bitcoin without raising a red flag since you don't have the mark, but maybe we could barter bread for wages. The black market is alive and well," said his uncle.

"How do you get along without the mark, Uncle Ben?"

"Most subjects of the Realm could care less about the mark. In my case they know that production would slow, and the quality would suffer. No one seems to want to learn anything. All they care about is whether the Beast gets his bread, and they get their daily dose of the Amy. I pay dearly for my freedom in graft to all levels of the government mandated employees. They always seem to have their hand out."

Two armed men burst into the room. Ben raised his palm to them, and their attitude changed.

"Just a misunderstanding, men, there is no need for the alarm."

They looked around puzzled, as if they saw an apparition.

Elezar's uncle waived them out the door just as his assistant came in with the reports. He introduced her to Elezar.

"Wanda, this is my nephew Elezar. Elezar, this is my right-hand assistant, Wanda. She is very zealous when it comes to my safety!'

She looked him up and down and finally acknowledged him. Benjamin ushered his nephew into his office to get caught up on old times.

As soon as they shut the door Benjamin put his finger to his lips signaling Elezar to be quiet. Benjamin pointed out the listening devices. Elezar nodded.

As Benjamin made small talk, he wrote down an address and a meeting time and handed the paper to Elezar. They talked of family for a while, lamenting the death of everyone they were close to.

Elezar asked if he could see the factory operations. Ben's eyes lit up as he talked shop to Elezar.

He got out of his chair and led Elezar through the door. He checked in with his assistant.

"We're going to tour the operation. Wanda, I'll be back in two hours." He smiled at her and left through the double doors leading to the factory.

Elezar was getting dizzy and weak from the heat the bread making produced. Benjamin led him to the break room, sat him down at one of the tables and cut a piece of the bread in the middle of the table. After spreading some jam on it he handed it to Elezar.

Elezar couldn't remember anything ever tasting as good as that piece of bread. He tried to eat it slowly and savor it, but his hunger overruled, and he wolfed it down. His uncle prepared another slice as Elezar finished the first. Benjamin got up and poured Elezar some tea out of a container in the fridge.

"This is heavenly, Uncle!" managed Elezar between bites.

Benjamin smiled at him knowingly. "That is why they let me continue here without harassing me. They took over the factory and banished me for a while, but the bread quality suffered, so I made them a deal. They leave me alone, and I make the bread to the Beast's liking. It's a win-win for everybody," he paused. "How are you feeling now Elezar?"

"Much better, Uncle, I feel like I could continue the tour."

"Good! Follow me."

The two continued on until the factory was familiar to Elezar. They parted company at the front entrance and agreed to meet at the spot Ben had stipulated in his note. Ben slipped Elezar a loaf of the wonderful bread when they embraced. Elezar did his best to hide it under his shirt and arm.

Elezar headed back to his lair to hide his bounty and wait for the appointed time specified in his uncle's note. He spent his time rummaging in the abandoned apartments for anything he could use to survive.

Anything of any value had been looted long ago but he was looking deeper for small things they might have missed, like cans of food in a cupboard, or kitchen utensils, clothes that fit, all the small things that matter when starting over with absolutely nothing.

He hid his treasures in a void between the floor joists and pulled his makeshift bed over the opening. When the time came, he headed to the rendezvous point and waited. He spied his Uncle Ben strolling down the sidewalk and waited. When his uncle acknowledged him, he fell into step without saying a thing.

They walked in silence. Elezar noticed Ben's eyes scanning the surroundings, darting to and fro, up and down. Elezar looked at him puzzled.

"You will learn in time to check for cameras and spies before you speak. You will learn or you will die," Ben said matter-of-factly.

Ben was carrying a duffle bag. When he was convinced it was safe, he ducked into a small room with only one door and one small window. Ben closed the door and opened the bag. He handed Elezar a lab coat like the ones the factory workers wore.

"I want you to wear this tomorrow to work. There is a small pocket sewn into the right wrist area."

Ben reached into his vest pocket and produced a small composite card with what looked like a barcode on it and handed it to Elezar.

"Put this card in the sleeve pocket so the barcode faces out. This card mimics the mark and our internal factory security so you can get in safely. Security requires that you place your wrist in the code reader. That will get you past the guards. You will have to swipe it again when you get to the door of your quality control workstation."

Ben handed the duffel and the card to Elezar. He put the card in the secret compartment underneath his belt and zipped the coat back in the duffel.

"You will also find a false lining inside the coat. It is purposely made to hold loaves of bread. Your job is to pull a random loaf of bread as it comes down the cooling line before it is wrapped for distribution. You are to cut it open and examine the texture and the size of the yeast holes in the bread, weigh it, and smell and taste it.

After it passes the tests, it is discarded as damaged goods that can't be sold. Some of it goes to the break rooms but most of it was smuggled out the door by the last person that wore the vest. He got greedy and got caught by the police selling it to people who didn't have the mark. He disappeared without a trace leaving me shorthanded. Don't make the same mistake."

"I won't Uncle." Elezar replied.

"I'm counting on you to get as much of the bread as you can to people who are resisting the mark. Barter for what you need but never turn a hungry person away."

Elezar never knew this side of his uncle. His father only told him of the businessman. The wealthy, ruthless, make a profit at all costs businessmen. Ben sensed the puzzled response.

"I'm sure you have only heard bad things about me from your father. When the Holy Spirit entered my life, I changed. I have found peace. That is why I carry on, showing others the Way through kindness. When the chance came for me to leave this misery and go with all the other believers I refused. I knew

God has put me here and provided me with a means to make a difference in the lives of many through this bakery and you!"

"But Uncle! I don't even believe in God! When father died, I cut my locks and my ties to his religion. I can't believe in a God that allows so much misery, and death, and sadness!"

Ben smiled at Elezar's retorts.

"First of all, God will use whoever he wants. Second, how did you survive when they came for your father? They usually kill everyone in the family just for sport. I see the wound on your head. You fought with them, didn't you? That gives them cause in their minds to kill you, but they didn't. Why?"

Elezar had no answers for his uncle. He pondered what his uncle said while they walked. They came to a cross street and Ben stopped.

"This is as far as I go. I will see you tomorrow at eight sharp. I will check in on you and train you myself. I want you to think about ways to get the bread out the door and into the hands of those who need it. I'm counting on you. Your contact is Frieda Ben-Ezra. She will find you. By the way, check the bottom of the duffel when you get home."

Ben turned around and walked back the way he came. Elezar stood still in contemplation for a few minutes watching his uncle walk away. He didn't really want to get mixed up in his uncle's intrigue, he had enough problems just trying to survive, but what choice did he have? He'd already had enough of scrounging for the meager scraps left in the endless war of attrition waged by the Realm. The shadows were getting long as he walked back to his squatter's palace.

He hesitated before he walked up the stairs to his den. His eyes darted left and right, up and down looking for evidence of unwanted guests, animal or human. He climbed slowly with his knife drawn and ready. At the top of the stairs, he swept the area with his eyes until he was satisfied he was alone, a routine he would practice every day. His attention turned to the duffel he carried.

He pulled out the lab coat and found a pair of matching pants and a pair of slip-on footies he was to wear in the lab. Under that was a loaf of the leavened, unsliced bread his uncle was famous for, wrapped in the familiar wrapping with the logo of the company emblazoned on every inch. Under that bread was a container of a protein spread resembling peanut butter that was almost impossible to buy, even for those with the mark, and a flask of untainted water. He smiled at his uncle's thoughtfulness. It was nice to have family again.

2

The Contact

She found Ben's note left on the way back to his factory. Ben walked every day after work so no one would suspect his motives. The new contact was described to her in detail. When she read the part about him being Ben's nephew, she rolled her eyes. Nepotism sometimes complicated things. When a runner went rogue, they had to be dealt with. Her people couldn't afford to go without the sustenance the bread provided, nephew or not.

The last guy started to extort her people and get rich off of their misery. She made sure it didn't go on. She knew people that could put a stop to that kind of behavior.

She waited patiently until he came out to walk at break, like Ben instructed him, with his lab coat full of the bread. The loaves of bread were all the sustenance some of her people got during the day.

She became lost in thought, the new wealth was food, meat, bread, eggs, any edible staple. The scorching dryness brought on by the two prophets in the city had changed society to a primitive barter subsistence. Bitcoin wealth was worthless unless there was food to buy with it. The new elite were the farmers, the hunters and gatherers in the wilderness, and the bread makers... It wouldn't be long before this Elezar would appear. She would be ready.

A figure matching his description walked toward her. She came around the corner and walked past him to confirm. His white lab coat was the clincher. It was bulging with the bounty she was after.

"ELEZAR!" she exclaimed.

When he turned around, she flipped back her ever-present Monk's hood. He stopped and turned and froze. There before him was the most beautiful woman he'd ever seen. Her dark, almost black hair flowed down, trying its best to escape her hoodie. Her skin was olive perfection, and her dark eyes mirrored the passion that oozed from her every movement. She was saying something to him, but he was caught up in her charm and didn't hear.

"Huh?" he managed.

"I SAID follow me!" She commanded.

He complied, not taking his eyes off her smooth, fluid body as she led the way.

She led them to a mostly intact house through an alley. She opened the door and slipped in with him close behind.

As soon as the door closed, she said, "Let's have it!"

He unbuttoned and held his coat open as wide as he could. She immediately started unloading his bounty. His face turned red. It crossed his mind that he looked like a flasher with that pose and immediately started to take off his garment.

At the same time, in her zeal to get all the loaves, Frieda reached behind him for a loaf in the back of the robe and got her arms tangled behind him. They struggled to free themselves of each other, Elezar only half-heartedly. He breathed her essence as they struggled. He freed his coat and held it in front of him for her convenience.

"Sorry, "he said with a sheepish grin.

Their eyes met briefly, and he was frozen in time. She reached for the remaining loaf of bread and tucked it away.

"You better get back. Your break will be over soon."

"Yeah, I better get back," he said, not wanting to go.

She turned and disappeared out the door. By the time he recovered enough to follow with his eyes, she was gone. Disappointed, he moved on back to his new job. The more he walked, the more he realized he would see her at least four times a day, morning break, lunch, afternoon break, and after work. His face lit up and he was grinning from ear to ear.

Frieda tried not to think of the new contact. She couldn't, she wouldn't get involved! Still his dark flowing hair and dark eyes moved her and stayed in her mind. She had to be aloof and ready so this rookie wouldn't mess up what she had worked so hard to accomplish.

The main thing was the bread pipeline was flowing again. She was not going to let her attraction to this guy get in the way! Hundreds were counting on her for a daily subsistence living.

When he walked by next time, she was ready. He didn't have to be coaxed this time. He knew exactly where to go. When he saw her, he smiled a silly schoolboy smile and his eyes lit up.

She moved like a cat pouncing on prey. The sleeves of her garment fell back revealing two nasty looking knives she positioned close to his neck. Her knives forming a "V" with his Adam's apple the center point.

"If you move backward these knives dig into your throat! If you move forward, these knives cut your Jugular. If you stand still and listen, you live."

"I'm listening," he calmly replied. He wasn't afraid, he was enamored.

She couldn't understand why she was so enraged at this guy. What happened was a misunderstanding on her part. She was more afraid of her own feelings than threatened by him, but she couldn't help herself. She had to set him straight!

"The last guy that tried to rape me got his kidneys cut out." She moved one knife away so he could see the way it was mounted.

She still had nightmares about the assault even though she was in the right and only protecting herself.

She moved the knife back toward him. It was mounted like a shark fin against her wrist. A flick of her wrist moved it across his body. The knife protruded like a grappling hook, the end stopping just before it drew blood.

The sawtooth edge would pull the knife deeper as she pulled her wrist across the body, making the hapless victim who struggled and thrashed dig the knife deeper until the struggle was over.

"You deliver bread! That's it!!" You ever touch me again I'll cut your heart out!"

"I deliver bread." He said, "Got it!"

The knives disappeared back in the protective sheath in her hoodie sleeves. She wouldn't look him in the eyes.

"Take the coat off and hand it to me!" she demanded.

He complied, still with that silly grin on his face.

She emptied his coat of the loaves and threw it back to him.

"Get out!"

He did, but he knew he would be back in a few hours.

The third encounter went without incident because they didn't talk. He handed her the lab coat, and she took the bread and tossed his coat back and left. He went back to work.

The day flew by. He couldn't get her out of his mind even though she did threaten to kill him! His final chance to see her for the day filled his thoughts. He wondered if she would go ballistic again if he asked about her family.

I think I'll risk asking her. What can she do but kill me! He thought, knowing in the back of his mind she wouldn't.

"I'm going to marry her some day!" he said under his breath to himself, "That is, if she doesn't kill me first!" he laughed out loud.

His shift ended and he headed out the door toward the rendezvous point in anticipation.

When he ducked into the doorway she was waiting. He shed his coat and handed it to her. While she worked, he puffed up his courage.

"You got any family?" he asked; A round-about way to see if she was married.

She didn't stop work but finally said, "No."

" All I have is Uncle Ben. My father was killed a few days ago and he was all of my immediate family left." He volunteered

"I know," she said without looking up.

"How do you know," he asked.

"I make it my business to know who I let into my life and my operation."

"I am at a disadvantage then because I know nothing about you."

"You'll learn on a need-to-know basis." She said matter-of-factly as she threw his coat back at him.

He caught his coat, put it on.

"See you tomorrow!"

He walked out of the building and down the street toward his squatter's quarters. He caught a glimpse of Frieda and another woman heading the other way.

3

The Colony

Weeks went by with the same routine. Sometimes, she even smiled at him when he walked in, well, at least she didn't frown. Things were thawing slightly; she walked over and handed his coat to him now instead of throwing it at him and actually started carrying on a conversation occasionally. She seemed more receptive to him since he did his job so well day after day and didn't hit on her constantly.

"What do you do after work?" she asked on day.

"Mainly I scrounge for food or go down and listen to the Prophets talk. Then I go home and sleep and wake up and come to work."

For the first time since they met, she looked him in the eye.

"I need your help."

She couldn't keep the pleading out of her voice. She didn't want to keep the pleading out of her voice.

She continued, still looking him in the eye, "One of my operatives got caught yesterday by the soldiers. She was dead by morning. She took the poison capsule we all carry so she couldn't talk. They do unspeakable things to women when they catch one with no mark."

"What did she do for you?"

"She helped distribute the bread you bring us and any other food our contacts can get. There is always more need than food. The ones with the mark can't buy enough so it's almost impossible for us."

"Sure, I'll tag along, probably more exciting that what I had planned."

At the end of his shift, after the bread was removed from his coat for the last time he hung around.

"What do we do now?"

"We wait. When it gets close to dark, we will deliver the bread. It's about five Kilometers to the safe house. We try to time our travels so the patrols are winding down and before the jackals come out."

"Jackals?"

"Yes, that's what we call the people who come out at night and hunt for food and anything they can pilfer. They are even known to cannibalize their victims when times are lean, like now."

"Safe house?"

"Yes, it's where people without the mark come to get a little something to help them survive the famine and drought. This one is The Clal Center, off of Jaffa Rd, bordering Kiah and Agrippa St. The high rise was abandoned and the mall is empty. The underground parking garage is intact and secure, so we stay there. We can only access it from Kiah. The elevators are shut down, but we have the stairs guarded and secure at all times. We have a colony of people without the mark that stay there."

"Yes, that's at least five kilometers from here," he said.

She looked him in the eyes and said with a grin, "Then we had better get started."

She picked up the military style duffel bag with half the bread bounty for the day and pointed at the other one. He picked it up without a word and secured it to his back like a soldier preparing for a hike.

"Lead the way!"

She led down dark alleys, through shadowy doorways, and around ominous corners like a cat on the prowl, her senses heightened to the least noise or movement. She set a pace a drill sergeant would envy. He struggled at times to keep up, but his male pride wouldn't admit it.

He was breathing hard under his breath, trying not to let her know. He was grateful when she motioned them to stop.

A patrol of troopers was crossing the path they needed to take. He froze. He didn't see them. He almost said something cute to her jokingly that would have given their position away. He shook his head in disgust at himself. When they were out of sight, he got on his feet to continue but she pulled him down.

Protecting the rear of the patrol were two troopers sweeping the area. He froze and rolled his eyes. Twice in less than two minutes he'd almost given them away. He was really impressed with her survival skills. He would trust her with his life in any situation. He just did.

He was still recovering when she disappeared around the corner and across the street. He adjusted his pack on the run. He recognized the streets. They were almost to Kiah. She disappeared into what looked like a pile of rubble against a building. It turned out to be a hidden stairway down to the former parking garage. He followed her down, his feet hitting each step sounded like a drum roll.

He was totally unprepared for what he saw. The walls of the dimly lit, cavernous room were lined with humanity. Couples, single men, single women, and families with children; they all had the same expression of hunger, helplessness, and fear, with that glimmer of hope that all humans have to have to survive.

They all had the gaunt sunken features of the nearly starved. When they saw Frieda, they began in unison to queue up by the long table where she was preparing to dole out each ration of bread.

He stood speechless at the shear enormity of the task she was undertaking.

"Hey, hot shot! You gonna help or stand there and be part of the problem!?"

He grabbed a knife and started slicing the bread just as she was. Each person got a portion according to their size and physical condition. Pregnant women got a double portion. He couldn't help but be energized just being close to her, feeling the passion she had for these people. The whole room was brighter just because she was there.

When the bread was gone Frieda collapsed into one of a group of chairs lining the wall. She motioned for him to sit in the one next to her. He settled into his gingerly, letting out a sigh as his body relaxed into the chair, his muscles grateful for the support. He leaned his head back against the wall next to her, still in awe of what she was capable of. He had pangs of guilt about his selfish "me first" attitude. He was certain he would be able to survive, but he never gave a thought to the thousands who were unable to survive on their own.

They didn't talk for a long time. The adrenalin, the stress, and the fatigue had to mellow before either could speak. He noticed a family across the room. They bowed their heads in unison and prayed before anyone ate. The father took out a cloth wrapped bar of dried and pressed fish and carefully broke off a small portion for each family member to eat with the bread. They each had a small flask of liquid to wash down the bread. Elezar wondered where they got the water and food and what they had to do to get it. He knew that type of food was for the ones with the mark.

As each one ate their ration they settled in for the night. The children seemed to go to sleep immediately after the hunger in their bellies was stilled. A mother shared her meager ration with her two boys. Elezar wanted to give her more but there was nothing left. He felt guilty about having his loaf and jam stash back at his squatter's inn.

"Do they stay down here all the time?" he finally asked.

"No," Frieda replied, "they work the greenhouses in the daytime. Some of the men go out and hunt for anything they can find."

"Greenhouses?"

"Yeah, the upper floors of the high rise are still intact and stable. The sides that get the sun are lined with gardens with every kind of edible plant we could find to grow. The hardest part is keeping enough water on the plants. We get water out of the Artesian well and pull it up in buckets through the elevator shaft. It is a long slow process. We barter our harvest for other foodstuffs and supplies when we have it. Of course, we preserve and dry as much as we can."

"The well appeared in a fracture in the concrete wall along the lowest level of the garage shortly after we occupied the building. We were desperate for water to drink and water for our plants when it happened. God had to have sent it. There is no other explanation."

He blew off the remark about God.

Each to his own beliefs he thought.

"So that is where the family across from us got the nutrition bar. He bartered for it."

"Yep," she replied.

"I gotta go! I have to be at work in a few hours."

"Why don't you stay here with us? We can find you a cot and some blankets. It's dark now and the streets aren't safe. I can't afford to lose you right now."

He nodded. He wished she needed him for him and not his uncle's bread, maybe in time. He was grateful for the secure place to sleep. She was right; the night belonged to the jackals.

He could see the gratitude in the eyes of the ones that set up his bed. They hugged him with thank you tears in their eyes.

His heart broke. He decided then and there he would do whatever he could to help these suffering people. As soon as his head hit the makeshift pillow he was out.

For the first time in a long time, he woke refreshed. He didn't have the recurring nightmare of the day his father was taken, like he did most nights. This place felt more like home than any place since his childhood.

The best part was when Frieda came over and told him they should get moving. She seemed to treat him differently now that he knew her secrets.

He didn't have anything except his lab coat and the empty duffels to take so they were off as fast as they came. The sun greeted them as they broke through the entrance. His spirit soared. He was with the only person in the world he wanted to be with. Happiness is a relative thing. For the first time in his recent memory, he could say he was happy.

They approached the bakery and split up. She went the back way into the abandoned house, and he slowed to a walk and approached the bakery like he always did.

When he cleared security and got to his workstation his uncle was waiting on him.

"I see you have been to the operation." Ben said.

"How would you know that by just looking at me?" Elezar retorted.

"I can tell by the smile on your face and the fire in your eyes that comes from enlightenment. Besides I talked to Freddie last week and set it up." Ben chuckled.

"Freddie?"

"Yes, that's my pet name for her. She's something else, isn't she?"

Ben was baiting Elezar to find out his feelings about Frieda.

"You can say that again!"

Ben smiled; he learned exactly what he needed to know by Elezar's enthusiasm.

"That's quite an operation she has isn't it." Ben handed Elezar a fresh lab coat as he talked, like he did every day, but he lingered this day.

"I had no idea why she was so passionate about the bread. I thought she was selling it on the black market!"

"I need to warn her and you now that you are part of the group. I eavesdropped on my "secretary" yesterday. The Realm is going to double patrols in order to eradicate—her words—the "Terrorists" that operate in this area of the city. The extra patrols will go until night fall every day for a month. Tell Freddie to be alert!"

"OK, I will, and Uncle, Thank you for this opportunity. I didn't know how bad it was out there until last night."

Ben smiled and nodded in acknowledgement. *There is hope for the future!* He thought as he went back to his rounds.

Elezar went about his business deep in thought. He could do this job now without even thinking. He started packing his special lab coat with the contraband bread as soon as the first batch of his shift came by. All he could really think of was Freddie. He was going to call her that when he saw her just to get her reaction!

His day flew by since he knew he would be going back to the group again. For the first time in his young life, he had a deeper purpose than self. The duffels were loaded, and they were ready to depart when he remembered what his uncle had said about extra patrols.

"Freddie, be careful tonight, Uncle said he heard that there would extra patrols roaming the streets until nightfall."

"I see you and your uncle have been talking. What did he tell you?"

"Nothing, just that Freddie was his name for you; Is it Ok if I use it too?"

"Yes, but I only let my close friends use it!"

His male incompetence with women showed through... All he could think of was to give her a high five when a hug would do. His spirit soared.

"I've got your back but don't take any chances today. Let's get there safe and sound." She was out the door before he finished his spiel. He shook his head at her nonchalant attitude and followed her out the door.

They followed one of the now familiar routes. They never took the same route twice in sequence for security. They had stopped for a patrol about half-way to their destination. Freddie (as Elezar now called her) hesitated and waited. When the second patrol bringing up the rear passed, she bolted out the door. Elezar was looking out a side window of the room and didn't see her leave. When he turned around, she was gone! He bolted out the door and immediately froze.

One trooper had Freddie pinned against the wall while the other checked her backpack.

"What have we here?" he said with an evil chuckle. "Looks like she don't have the mark."

"Look what she got in the bag, brother! It's the Beast's favorite bread! Looks like we hit the jackpot tonight! We'll get a good bounty for the girl and that bread is worth a fortune on the streets."

These were the worst kind of troopers, bounty hunters, the dregs of the marked society. They were criminals before the mark but now they had legitimacy; Legitimized Jackals out early on the prowl, pressed into service in sweeps like this one. The Realm used them to terrorize the neighborhoods into compliance. Most of them would turn in their own mothers if they thought they would get paid.

The one that had Freddie pined against the wall, grabbed her around the neck and forced her head against the building. He was much bigger than her and much stronger.

"I'm goin' to have a little fun with this sweet thang before we turn her in!"

He reached in to try and kiss her on the mouth, but she brought her left hand to his left side and her right hand to his right side in his soft belly. He felt the knives cut his flesh and tried to move away. When he did, she pulled her wrists across his body. The saw blade teeth pulled the knives in deep like a serpent's fangs.

The look on his face went from evil lust, to surprise, to pain in an instant. She watched as the life left his face. The main artery was severed in his abdomen. He had seconds to live. He released her face and seemed to fall in slow motion while his brother looked on bewildered.

She pulled with all her strength and the knives ripped free, dripping with the red karma due the evil life he had led.

The blood spewed like a fountain all over the pavement out of his brother's skewed abdominal cavity. Wide eyed, he took a second to process what just happened.

He turned his weapon towards Freddie and aimed.

Elezar saw what was going on. He felt sorry for the man facing Freddie. It was the other one he was worried about. He dropped his backpack instantly and checked for any more soldiers. He ran the twenty meters to Freddie as silently and as fast as he could. When the bounty hunter drew his weapon on Freddie Elezar's knife came out of its sheath and flew in the air like a guided missile.

The jolt snapped the man's head sideways. He dropped his weapon, but before he could fall, Elezar was upon him. Elezar's left land gripped the knife sticking out of the man's ear, his right arm grabbed the man's head in a head lock. His left hand shoved the knife in further and twisted it free. A trail of blood followed the bounty hunter to the ground, his head sounding like a dropped melon when it hit the pavement.

Elezar stood over him momentarily to make sure he was dead before he turned his attention to Freddie. She was leaning over, hands on her knees, with her backside still against the wall and her head down.

"You OK?" He said, pulling her up.

She grabbed him around the neck and held on, sobbing. He'd like to stay that way forever but knew they didn't have much time. He gently pulled her away and dried her eyes. She sensed his strength and became Freddie again. She would have to melt down later, hopefully in his arms.

"I'm going to drag these bodies into the alley so they can't be readily seen from the street. ..."

"Will you get my pack? I dropped it in the house we were in to come after you," He asked.

Instantly she complied.

While she was gone, he returned to the bodies and cut out the chip and the mark from each one. They wouldn't be using it anymore, he reasoned.

Freddie got back just as he finished with the last body.

"What are you doing?" she asked, disturbed at his actions.

"Look," he said. "If the Realm discovers they are missing then the chips will be traced here. We are going to make use of these chips and spend all the bitcoin they have before they are missed. They won't need them anymore!"

What he said made sense, but she was still uneasy about having anything to do with the bounty hunters' flesh. Elezar grabbed the men's weapons and tucked them away under his lab coat.

They ran the rest of the way to the shelter, stopping only to deposit the two marks in an abandoned house so they couldn't be tracked to the shelter.

"Freddie and Elezar were both breathing hard when they arrived. They stopped just inside and dropped the packs with the bread and bent over with their hands on their knees, panting.

When Freddie caught her breath, she called out to the nearest woman. "Greta, do we have any clean hoodies in my size?"

Greta hustled off to the storehouse to see. When she returned with the closest thing they had, she noticed the blood on Freddie and Elezar.

"Are you two Ok?"

"Yes," replied Freddie.

Elezar shed his lab coat. It was spotted red. His clothes were protected from the blood. But he needed to wash.

"Greta, can you get someone to distribute the bread for us tonight? We have an errand to run... and I need a long-sleeved robe, if you have one," Elezar asked.

She nodded.

"I also need to talk to the men for a minute," said Elezar.

She nodded and hurried to gather all the men she could find.

Elezar and Freddie went to the artesian well to wash.

When they got back the men gathered around.

"We have a mission tonight and we need your help. We can, for a short time get goods from the Realm's Government store. I'm not going into the details but I'm going to go where the marked go. We have a short window of opportunity to do this, and we need your help moving the goods. We will have to do this tonight so there is risk of getting caught by the jackals. Anybody in?"

They all volunteered.

"I have two laser rifles. I will leave it up to you who get assigned to them."

He handed over the weapons that the two bounty hunters carried. All citizens of Israel, on their eighteenth birthday, were conscripted into the military before the One World Government, so he knew there would be no shortage of competent marksmen.

"I'm going to go to the Government store and get as many things as the two chips I stashed in an abandoned house can purchase. We'll have to go back and get them; I was afraid to bring them here in case they were tracked.

"I'm going to buy proteins of all kinds and flour, sugar, barley, and anything I can think of that we can share and that will keep down here. I don't know how many bitcoins are on each chip, but I'll buy until the code stops me. I'm open to suggestions along the way what would do the greatest good."

"We don't have much time to plan our getaway but I'm going to get the goods to the edge of the lighted parking lot, and you can take it from there. I know I can count on your experience and judgment."

"Let's go!"

They filed out through the nearly hidden exit that Elezar and Freddie always used. Elezar led the way with Freddie close behind. The posse spread out and flanked them. The night had set. The only lights now were the glow of the streetlamps at the store and in the neighborhood where the marked lived.

They moved like the shadows of night to the abandoned house where the chips were stashed, then headed for the store.

As the warehouse store came into sight Freddie and the rest stayed in the shadows. Only Elezar could get through security. He strapped one of the marks to his wrist and covered it with his long sleeve, then handed the other to Freddie.

"I'll be back for this later. It wouldn't be good for me to have both when I go through screening."

She took the chip and couldn't contain her concern. She wrapped her arms around his neck and gave him a passionate but short kiss.

"Be careful! Come back to me and you can have the rest of that kiss."

"You can count on it!" he replied, a little weak in the knees from the surprise.

He turned and walked nonchalantly to the chip reader and stuck his right hand under it, ready to bolt as soon an alarm went off. An electronic buzz released the turnstile. At least he was in the front door. He grabbed a shopping cart, swiped his wrist so he could use the cart for two hours, and started his search. The security guards milled around, bored, looking at their watches from time to time, counting the minutes until their shifts ended.

He started in the dried foods first. He ran the packages one by one over the chip on the back of his wrist until the small green light on the package came on. He went for proteins of all kinds. Dried fish, poultry, beef, and lamb, "just add water and heat," the packages said.

The shelves were getting bare because of the time of day and the drought. He went to a different section and bought dried dates and dried figs. The cart was full, and his chip still worked. He rolled it to the front of the store where a bored guard waved him through without looking up.

He strolled past the parking lot lights. As soon as he got to the darkened area beyond the men grabbed the goods and bolted. He turned around and returned. He filled the cart again and still the chip worked. He repeated a third time before the card was depleted. He found Freddie and swapped out the chip and returned for a fourth trip. The guards didn't question him or his motives. He was puzzled. He thought he would have to explain, at some point in time, his "shopping" mission.

His legs and back ached but he pushed on. He was actually glad when the second chip was depleted. He walked out of the warehouse for the last time to the designated spot. The goods instantly disappeared, and he returned the cart where it belonged, not out of civic duty; he knew it was chipped and would set off an alarm if it wasn't back at the designated time.

He walked into the shadows where Freddie was to collect the rest of his kiss. She ambushed him, throwing her arms around his neck. As soon as their lips met, she wrapped her legs around him and he melted into her. They would have stayed that way the rest of the night but one of the men nudged his shoulder.

"We need to go!" the man said.

Freddie reluctantly extracted herself from him. He didn't want to let go. They hustled away with the two remaining men charged with getting them home safe. The others were still stashing all the bounty from the night's raid. They took the chips back to an abandoned house. There would be patrols around everywhere if anyone reported the bounty hunters missing.

They ran through the darkness hand in hand, flanked by the two armed men, to the underground colony. When they got through the door the people cheered and danced around them like they were conquering heroes.

Elezar was more than a little embarrassed by it all and turned red in the face. Freddie grinned at her hero's reaction. The children wanted to hug him and the women to touch him. They were all celebrating the bounty that God had provided. Elezar just wanted to sit down and rest.

He finally got his chance. Freddie sat down beside him and watched the children play. Their laughter was the kind of music everyone missed in such hard, evil times. Elezar turned to Freddie.

"What do your people do when I have a day off?"

"He didn't tell you?" Freddie asked, not surprised.

Elezar looked at her puzzled. "Tell me what?"

"Your uncle takes your shift, and we have a team in place that delivers the bread here."

Elezar hesitated, soaking in the information, "How do you know my uncle so well? You seem to know more about my family that I do!"

"My father worked for him back when he thought of nothing but production and profit. Ben and my father were best friends. My family is, was, messianic Jews. My father had the office to the right of Ben's; he was Ben's vice president over procurement. He bought all of the ingredients that go into the bread. I used to play in the reception area while my father worked. My mother, Martha, used to have your job. That's before the Realm took over. That's where my father met my mother!"

"You said, "Back when Uncle Ben thought of nothing but profit? What changed?"

"Ben was an agnostic. He knew the ways of the Jews, His family practiced Haredi Judaism but his religion was his factory, and his god was money. My father told him of the love of Jesus and the personal relationship he could have with him. Your uncle converted at a great cost. His family disowned him, and we were all he had. The Realm took my father and mother in the first wave of Martyrs. Your uncle hid me so I would survive.

"My family was Haredi, but when my father died, I cut my Parot and walked away. It seemed so pointless. Look at all the suffering in this world! What God would allow this?" Elezar pondered out loud.

She took his hand and looked him in the eye.

"Humankind has brought this upon itself. God knew the outcome before Adam and Eve. We are now in the last days before God's Kingdom. You are off tomorrow, come with me and we'll listen, really listen to the two prophets."

He didn't care about listening to the prophets, but he'd go anywhere with her. The two talked well into the night. Their conversation danced in an intimate embrace; two turtle doves fluttering around in spring. She fell asleep on his chest. He carried her to her bed and found his. He slept a peaceful, restful sleep full of bright future dreams, despite his everyday reality.

Some of his dreams puzzled him, others made him smile. All of them involved Freddie.

For the first time in what felt like ages, his visions no longer revolved around the past.

4

First Date

The places a young couple could go to be together were very limited, especially ones who didn't have the mark. At least the Realm had given up trying to silence the Prophets. It was a sanctuary where the ones with the mark mingled with those who didn't have it, no questions asked.

Freddie and Elezar slipped out the front of the colony to a bright mid-morning sun. Instead of their usual hurried pace they strolled hand in hand in the general direction of the prophets, not in a hurry to get there. They didn't talk but said volumes, two souls melding into one.

Finally, he asked her, "Why were you so nasty to me when we first met?"

"She looked in his eyes, "I was afraid of you!" she replied sheepishly.

He looked at her puzzled.

"Not physically afraid of you, afraid of the way I felt about you."

He looked at her puzzled. He still didn't understand.

She continued, "I couldn't let anyone into my life at that point, especially a stranger. I had just lost a comrade in arms... my best friend. I lost my parents, and everyone I have ever known is dead or has disowned me because I wouldn't take the mark, except for Ben. I didn't want to put you in jeopardy by just knowing me! I couldn't let you get close. I couldn't stand another loss."

He put his arm around her and drew her closer.

"I get it. Ben is all I have left too!"

She looked at him puzzled. He didn't get it.

They walked in silence, enjoying their time together. When they got close enough to the crowd to hear the prophets, they stopped. Elezar and Freddie listened to the two and talked among themselves in hushed tones. Elezar didn't understand much of what they were saying. Freddie tried to explain their words were something that has to be felt, to an unbeliever who wasn't ready to feel.

Midafternoon, she produced a flask of water and some of the bread they risked their lives for every day of the week. She discretely broke off a piece and handed it to Elezar. They shared the water.

"I thought today was one for fasting?" he asked.

She smiled, "Greta pressed this into my hand before we left and just said, enjoy. She smiled and hugged me. How could I refuse?"

"I'm glad!" he said as he savored the treat.

They listened in silence. Freddie soaked it in, but Elezar was lost. He had heard of Jesus and knew he was a Jew, but his father didn't allow any views in his house but Haredi and his own.

The shadows were long when they decided to return to the compound. Tomorrow they would resume the fight, but for now they would enjoy their time. They slipped into the compound in the dark shadows. The children were fed, and the compound was settling into another rest.

Freddie went to her women's quarters and Elezar to his men's. Elezar fell asleep pondering the message he heard from the Prophets. His sleep was deep and tranquil, even though he seemed to dream all night. Like a video that he was aware of, but not part of. He longed to be part of it. Morning commitments intruded as they always do, and he prepared to meet Freddie at the entrance. She was there waiting. A nod and they were off.

"I want to go back the way we came the last time," he informed Freddie.

"OK," she replied without enthusiasm.

Freddie was in full trooper mode, looking right, left, scanning rooftops for cameras, and the sky for drones. They came upon the site where the altercation took place two days ago. Freddie stepped gingerly over the dark stains but didn't break stride.

The sooner they got past that spot the better! She thought. She didn't look back to see if Elezar was behind her.

Elezar hesitated long enough to check to see if the bodies were still there. The only evidence was a pile of bones and entrails covered with flies and the makeshift tripod, where the harvest took place. The Jackals feasted that night!

He caught up with Freddie in the house they always use for a safe haven to catch their breath.

"Did you find them?" she asked.

"Yeah, they're there."

He didn't mention the rest to her.

That explains why the death wagons never came to collect the dead like they used to! He thought.

They never took that route again.

They rounded the last corner and ducked into the house. Elezar shed the backpack, turned to Freddie, kissed her goodbye, and walked into the morning sunlight toward the factory as if the weekend was just a figment of his imagination.

Freddie would scout the area and prepare for their evening run.

Greta had tried her best to get the bloodstains out of his lab coat. He could only hope that the guard was his usual inattentive self and wouldn't notice the residue. He knew his uncle would be in with a fresh coat in a few minutes. Elezar had so many questions for his uncle about the Prophets' message.

The first batch of bread came out of the oven onto the huge conveyer, so Elezar settled in for the morning's routine. Ben walked in as he was finishing his testing and handed him his fresh coat. Elezar swapped out the coat immediately.

"I see you had a little accident this weekend," he said.

"Yes, a little trouble with some zealous bounty hunters."

"I hope it was resolved favorably," was all Ben said.

His attitude made Elezar wonder if he already knew all about it.

"I went with Freddie to listen to the Prophets this weekend. I had heard them before but never really stopped to listen. I have many questions and you are the only person I can trust to answer them truthfully without getting arrested.

Ben smiled knowingly. Elezar suspected Ben already knew his questions before he even asked. It was a bit unnerving! Ben produced a small device that looked like a hearing aid.

"Wear this in your ear as you sleep. It will answer your questions and bring out more."

Ben reached back into his pocket and produced a paper with a splash of beautiful colors.

"When you are ready, a mural of our Christ will appear on this page when you touch it. Show it to Greta and she will introduce you to your mentor and teacher within the compound. He will guide you on your journey to redemption." Ben smiled and turned to leave.

Elezar had so many questions but when he spoke Ben put up his hand with his palm toward Elezar. Elezar forgot everything he wanted to ask!

I'm beginning to think there is more to Uncle Ben than anyone is aware of, thought Elezar. He returned to his tasks, pondering Ben's actions.

At the morning break, Elezar was out the gate as usual. He had things he had to show Freddie. While she unloaded his bread he reached in his pocket and produced the paper that his uncle had given him.

When she turned around and saw the paper, she grabbed her heart like women do when they are being proposed to! She touched the paper gently while tears welled in her eyes. She wanted so badly for him to know what she knew. Now he would get the chance. She was an empath with some powers also, but her power fell short of the Master. She knew Elezar was strong in passion, but he denied the existence of the very God who pursued him.

She could only kiss him and push him on his way before she buried her head in her hands and wept for joy. She wouldn't see him much for the duration of the training but that was a sacrifice she was willing to make.

5

Training

Elezar finished the day as usual but anxiously anticipated the chance to meet this Mentor that Ben talked about. He talked to Freddie about his experience with Ben that morning. She excitedly told him about the ones so strong in the Faith that they held the power to alter the outcome of events under insurmountable circumstances. The Masters they were called. The ones called by God to protect His Remaining Kingdom until His return.

The bread was distributed and the people settling down for the night. Elezar touched the paper in his pocket. Nothing happened. He walked over to Greta and handed it to her. She smiled as if she was expecting him and nodded her head and disappeared before he could explain! It was frustrating to Elezar to not be in the "loop", or not know what was going on. It seemed like everyone he approached was already in on the plan but him!

Elezar had never seen the tall, thin, unassuming man that approached him in a dark full-length robe. The hood of the robe moved to reveal a white haired, gentle mannered man, whose dark eyes captivated Elezar.

He felt a peaceful power emanate from the man. At first Elezar wasn't sure if he was even human! The man had a strange strawberry mark on his forehead that looked like a thumbprint.

Elezar's eyes were drawn to the mark. He didn't mean to stare rudely but it was so unusual. The man took no offense.

"It is the mark of the King. I am set apart. My lineage is from the tribe of Judah. I am one of twelve thousand chosen from the clan." He said matter-of-factly.

"How can you possibly know that? The records were lost thousands of years ago in the many times God banished us from the land!" Elezar chided.

"I did not know, but my lord and Master did. He knows the hairs on my head. My power comes from my Faith in Him. Walk with me."

"But it is dark out! It is too dangerous to be out there now. I've seen what the Jackals do to people out when the sun goes down!"

"Ah, but the Son never leaves; He is only hidden by our darkness!" said the stranger with a wry smile.

He headed for the exit and Elazar shrugged and followed, shaking his head.

"Hey! What's your name?" he asked when he caught up to him.

"Abijah, you may call me Abe."

"Why did you choose me? I don't know anything about your Jesus or any of the things the Prophets say."

"But your heart is good, and your mind is free."

"Free of what?"

"Free. Free to choose."

Elezar was deep in thought when he saw the band of street thugs, jackals, coming toward them. His knife was out instantly, and he instinctively jumped in front of the old man to protect him. The gang started running toward them and surrounded them, taunting them, menacing them. Abe quietly raised his palm and the men fell silent, bewildered.

Abe walked away with Elezar still brandishing his weapon, keeping his body between the men and Abe. The men acted like they no longer saw the pair and turned and headed away from Elazar and Abe as if they were invisible.

Bewildered at the thugs, Elezar put away his knife. He walked in stride with Abe, glancing over his shoulder to make sure the gang didn't ambush them from behind. The thugs faded into the darkness.

They walked in silence for a while, Elezar wondering if he imagined the altercation.

"What just happened back there?" Elezar demanded.

"Many look but few see; many hear but few listen." Abe replied with a sly smile. "What do you think happened?"

"I thought we were about to get robbed and killed. Why did they just stop like that?"

"They no longer saw us in their reality..." He smiled again. "Where were we? Ah yes, why you were chosen." Abe continued as if nothing happened. "When you first brought the bread to the colony what did you do?"

"I helped to distribute it." Elezar answered.

"Why did you do that for someone you didn't know? Why did you decide to make their survival your passion? Why did you defend Frieda when she was in need?"

"I don't know why! I just thought they were the right things to do!"

"Your father raised you well. He instilled in you discipline, discernment, respect, and the value of works, but he rejected the Way. I want to offer you the power to heal, to move mountains, and most of all to move people. I have only the Faith of a mustard seed, but I can do all these things through Christ!"

Elezar pondered these things. He had so many questions, "Who is this Jesus that you talk of? What makes him so powerful?"

"He is the way, the truth, and the life. He is the strength in your body you claim for your own." "The device that Ben handed you is a receiver. You can hear the Prophets simply by putting it in an ear. God sent them to save the Jews who will receive His message and repent in the end times.

"You have suffered the rants of an old man enough for the night. Listen to the prophets as much as you can and meet me tomorrow, if you are intrigued; we can talk."

"We must return to the compound."

Elezar walked with Abe in silence. He had so many questions. He didn't know why he was drawn to this man or to the Jesus he talked about. He needed to talk to Freddie when they got back to the compound.

She was waiting excitedly for him when he got back.

"Are you going to go through the mentoring?" She asked.

"Yes, I can't quit now! I have so many questions."

"We won't be able to see one another as much as we do now. I talked to Ben this morning about filling in for you. He said he would for as long as the training takes. Did you know that Ben went through the training?"

"No, but that explains a lot. I had a lot of questions for him, but he raised his hand, and I couldn't remember a single one! He also seems to be able to go anywhere without being questioned. If he is as good as Abe, you will be in safe hands while I'm gone."

"Oh, he is but in a different way. He is like me, an empath!"

They talked into the night about his questions and things that young couples talk about. He escorted her to her section in the compound where they said their goodbyes. Sometimes, that takes as long as the conversations, when two people are in love.

When he got to his cot, he put the receiver that Ben gave him in his ear and spent the remainder of the night in vivid dreams of places and events from the past. He seemed to be a passive intruder, a spirit that saw but could not be seen. He woke rested, at peace. He hurried to catch Freddie before she left. It seemed odd for her to leave without him. They kissed and he watched as she hustled out of sight.

When he turned to go in Abe was standing in the doorway.

"So, you want to learn the Way?"

Elezar was taken aback. He hadn't confided in anyone except Freddie about his decision.

"How do you know these things?" he asked Abe

"The Holy Spirit guides me, and my Master grants me insight into such things."

"Please follow me so we can get started."

Elezar followed him into the compound and up a stair into the high rise. The old man seemed to manage the steps effortlessly. After the fifth floor Elezar's legs were starting to get heavy, but he pressed on.

Finally, on the tenth floor the old man opened the door into a cavernous, empty room. Their footsteps echoed in the emptiness.   Elezar spotted two wooden chairs facing each other. Abe motioned him to sit in the chair opposite him.

"Where would you like to begin?"

Elezar didn't hesitate.

"At the beginning!"

"There is no beginning. God has always been. His creation will always be."

Elezar was frustrated at Abe's response.

"What is the beginning for me?"

"Your "beginning" was known to God when he created Adam and Eve. You are but an infinite ripple in the waves of time. Your earthly existence is a test, a winnowing, separating the good grain from the chaff."

"How do I become the grain and not the chaff?"

"You choose. For instance, the two men that meant Frieda harm chose the world and the temporary pleasures that it represents. They sold their Godly birthright for the things of this world with contempt for what He offered. They too will live forever but in the absence of God."

"Unfortunately, this must be. The universe exists in opposing waves of good and evil. Just like heat tempers cold, good tempers evil. We are created with the capacity for both and must choose one or the other. Satin has only the power that we give him!"

Elezar's mind was racing. He was digesting what the old man said. He didn't speak for a few minutes.

"What if I choose the Way and do something that displeases God?"

"We have Grace. I repeat, we are being winnowed like grain, so the evil falls to the threshing floor."

Elezar contemplated. An embarrassed smile crossed his lips as he spoke.

"The only people I know that embrace the Way are you and Uncle Ben and neither of you are married. Is that a requirement for service to the Way?"

"No, and you are mistaken. Everyone in the compound embraces the Way. It is not for a select few."

"Then why can't they do what you are capable of doing?"

"We are all given gifts to use in His service. We are judged by how we use those gifts, not by what the gifts are. They are equally important in the Creators plan.

Elezar again was silent. He got out of his chair and paced.

"I have to know; how did you manipulate those men? I thought sure we would have to fight our way out of that mess."

Abe smiled and raised his hand and disappeared from Elezar's perception. Elezar actually went to the chair Abe was sitting in and waved his hand around in disbelief!

"Where are you?!"

"Look behind you!" Abe said.

"How did you do that?"

"God's time. I'm sure you have heard people say, "In God's time"."

"God's time is not measured in seconds, minutes, hours, or days. That is Human measurement. God's time cannot be measured. His time is layers, or waves, that He controls so that situations meet, not minutes. He has given some of us a very limited gift of manipulating the waves of time closest to us. I merely raised the veil of another time and we slipped by them unnoticed. My power is very limited. Can you imagine mankind having free reign of the time waves? It would be total chaos."

"God has stymied geologists, paleontologists, physicists, and all others seeking truths by simply manipulating time so that the puzzle pieces, the answers they seek, never seem to come together."

"Why would he do that? Why shouldn't humankind have access to the pieces of the puzzle?"

"We have such a capacity for evil that some answers are kept from us because God knows they would be used for domination and exploitation. Look at the way the Beast has exploited the whole human race with the amygdaloideum. The knowledge was given to him by men bent on world domination and control of all wealth."

Elezar contemplated all that Abe revealed to him. His head was spinning with questions. "Who is this Jesus you call Master and what makes Him special?"

"He came as our Messiah, our hope and redemption. He was God in human form, but the evil of the Pharisees and Sadducees, whose power and authority he threatened, had Him crucified as a false prophet. The King of the world was laid to rest in a borrowed tomb. He rose on the third day to show all peoples that God knows their suffering and was willing to send His Son as a sacrificial lamb to take all sins with him."

"But why would an all-powerful, all-knowing God do that. Why didn't he intervene and punish the Pharisees and Sadducees?"

"Why did he not just take the Jews out of Egypt and place them in the Promised Land?"

"I don't know!" Elezar retorted.

"God knows our capacity for evil. He gives us free will to choose our destiny. We are given every chance to repent and choose him. He knew the hearts of the Israelites before he redeemed them from Pharaohs' grasp. They were winnowed to separate the true wheat from the chaff."

"We are in the final days of the End Times. We have many afflictions to endure before Armageddon, but the chosen will be delivered. God wants you to be among the chosen, but you must first choose Him!"

"You must first believe."

Elezar looked Abe in the eyes.

"I do believe; Lord God help my unbelief!"

"You must have faith that he will help your unbelief."

"As you make the transition you must die to self and clear your heart to allow Him to work!"

Elezar fell prostrate on the floor. A pure white light descended on him. He was transported past reality to a light that was more powerful than the sun. It engulfed him with gentle warmth. He was taken to the future and shown a city descending on the Earth bathed in the light.

Tranquility surrounded the Earth that had not been felt since the fall of Adam and Eve.

His body convulsed as he was pulled back from the tranquil light and shown the things the World would suffer. The entity radiating the light seemed to answer his questions before he spoke!

Abe was standing over him when he came to. He extended his hand to help Elezar to his feet. Weakness overcame Elezar and he collapsed in one of the chairs.

When he gained enough strength he asked Abe, "What was that?"

"That was the power of the Holy Spirit manifested in a vision. Jesus allowed you a glimpse into our future. The conversion of Saul into Paul in the book of Acts was similar, only Saul was temporarily blinded. He chose the Way. Will you?"

"I have never felt so much love and peace; my heart felt whole for the first time in my life!"

Abe smiled a knowing smile. "You are truly chosen by God. Will you choose him?"

"Yes! Yes! Yes!"

Elezar fell to his knees and worshiped. He felt strength and inner peace engulf him.

He understood what the Prophets were talking about for the first time. Although he had never read the Bible the Word of God was impressed in his mind. His transformation was complete!

"All that remains is submersion. The water signifies you have died and been reborn, cleansed of all past sin and ready for the Holy Spirit. Come, we must return to the group."

Abe led Elezar down the stairs. The steps came effortlessly to them as they glided to their destination. The door opened into the compound. All the people were there to greet them.

The whole place was bathed in the light Elezar was now familiar with. Freddie was the first to greet him. She gently touched his hair and caressed his face while looking deep into his eyes. She could feel his power and see his transformation!

'I've missed you so much since you've been gone! This was the longest week of my life."

She put both hands on his cheeks and pulled him in for a long kiss.

"Your hair is snow white!"

"I...I didn't know! How long did you say I've been gone?"

"A whole...long...week!" she replied kissing him between words.

"I felt no night or day! I thought I was gone a day."

He was stunned. He hadn't eaten or drank anything for a whole week, but he felt no hunger or thirst! What a God he now served! He thought.

"Why is everyone assembled tonight?"

"They are here for your baptism of course. It is a big event!"

They all made a path for the two to the artesian well. The joyous atmosphere was contagious. In normal times they would go to the River Jordan to baptize but that was an immediate death sentence if they were caught.

A trough large enough to submerge a man fashioned out of stones was lined with a vinyl tarp. The water gurgled and swirled in a pool at the end where the water flowed out of the wall and overflowed around the top of the trough spilling down the stone onto the floor. Abe positioned himself beside the water and motioned Elezar to enter.

"I baptize you in the name of the Father, The Son, and the Holy Spirit!"

Elezar barely heard the words before the water rushed over his face. The noise of the well-wishers muffled as he descended. He was under for a split second. He came out of the water shouting with his arms raised toward Heaven. The elation he felt was unmatched in his old secular world. He knew he was part of the Kingdom. He fell to his knees in prayer.

When he arose, the crowd gathered around to congratulate him. Freddie held back until the well-wishers drifted off. She handed Elezar the silicon paper. His face shone bright as the image of the Christ appeared! He was truly blessed.

6

Wedding Bells

Elezar and Freddie resumed their routine and delivered the bread daily. Elezar spoke daily with Abe, gaining knowledge, faith, and strength. The colony prospered because of Frieda and Elezar.

One evening, like any other evening, they were double-timing their way toward the compound with full loads of bread when Elezar saw a patrol near the entrance to the parking garage. One of the troopers stopped at the camouflaged entrance. He saw the worn path and the obvious attempt to hide the entrance. His handheld scanner didn't register anyone with the mark, so he knew he'd stumbled onto an unauthorized domicile. He motioned his comrades to investigate.

Elezar and Freddie froze. If the compound was discovered many innocent people would suffer and die. He dropped his bag and stood perfectly still, praying earnestly for guidance.

"Lift the veil!" a voice inside him said loudly.

Elezar glanced at Freddie to see if she heard it. She was still frozen in place.

He saw Abe do that on the first night he met him. Doubt crept into his psyche. He had never tried to warp time. What if he couldn't do it? What if he failed and the compound was discovered?

"LIFT THE VEIL!"

He heard it again! Without even thinking he raised both palms toward the entrance. He felt the wave move through his body just as the troopers entered the compound.

The patrol went one by one into the entrance. Then last trooper guarded the entrance, scanning the area for possible ambush. He looked directly at Elezar and Freddie but didn't react.

The boots of the soldiers inside made a hollow sound in the dusty, abandoned emptiness of the parking garage. The only light was the second-hand reflection of the evening sun sneaking its way down the elevator shaft through the broken doors. The only sounds beside the footsteps were the moaning of the high rise above as it argued with the wind. The only occupants were the spiders who built elaborate webs to trap intruding flies.

"Come on, let's get out of here," the platoon leader said.

All the troopers filed out the same way they went in. The one who discovered the entrance was the last to leave. Bewildered, he noted the weeds at the entrance only carried the scars of the soldiers as they moved through. He could have sworn the path was bare when they went in. He took the flask of Amy out of his vest pocket and took another hit.

I need some R&R, he thought to himself.

Elezar and Freddie hid in the dry brush growing around the building until the troopers disappeared in the distance. Freddie picked up her bread and sprinted into the compound with Elezar trying to keep pace behind her. When she burst into the parking garage the occupants wondered, why the sudden urgency? She looked around to an uninterrupted routine. She looked at Elezar puzzled.

"I'll explain later!" he said.

They went about the business of distributing the bread. They sat together resting from the day's labor. Elezar noticed that the people seemed to have more than just the bread now. Vegetables of all kinds complimented the dried meat and fish. The families sat around in a circle savoring the bountiful meals talking and laughing. He was taken back in his mind to a time when he was a child. These family times jostled his memory of better times. He smiled and let his head fall back against the wall with his eyes closed.

I need to start a family, he thought. Even in these harsh times the need was there.

His thoughts were interrupted by Freddy.

"What happened at the entrance to the compound today? I thought sure the soldiers were going to find us." Freddie asked.

"I sent then into a different time, God's time. It is one of the gifts he gave me at my conversion. I had never done it before, but I saw Abe do it the night I met him. I can move the waves of time closest to me to accomplish God's purpose, but I cannot use it for my own gain or to hurt anyone. I moved them in time to before the colony was established so they saw only an abandoned complex."

She looked deep into his eyes and her heart filled with joy at the man he had become.

"Can I change the subject?"

"Sure."

He took her hand and kissed the back of it. He slid out of the chair onto one knee.

"I knew the first time I saw you that someday I would marry you. I didn't know if I would live to ask you, but I have and I'm asking now. Will you marry me?"

She was stunned but she recovered quickly.

"Yes! I'll marry you!"

All the butterflies and anxiety left him! He stood and caught her in an embrace. Her feet left the floor as he twirled her around the room. The women in the room knew what had happened instantly but had to explain it to most of the men.

They all restrained until she made the formal announcement and then the two were mobbed by the well-wishers that, through adversity, had become their family.

When the furor died down, they embraced and kissed.

"I don't have any material gifts to give you." he said in a soft voice with his head down, "I don't even have a proper place to live."

"You have given me all I want and that is to be your wife."

She kissed him and then pushed him away with her palm on his chest. The women were already gathering to be part of the wedding planning and she needed to be with them.

"I've got to go now. I have a wedding to plan!"

Elezar sat down in his chair a little bewildered. The man whose family always ate their evening meal across from him came over and sat down beside him.

"You look a little lost, Elezar."

"I am Ezra. What just happened here?" asked Elezar.

Ezra smiled. "It happens every time. The women are so excited for her that they will all be pre-occupied with planning for a few days. She'll have a hundred questions that you will have no idea how to answer about colors, bridesmaids, groomsmen and other things you don't have a clue about or don't care about."

"Abe will be here shortly. He is qualified to perform the ceremony. You might ask him. Another thing, I know you and Frieda don't have family, except for Ben. Why don't you suggest to Frieda that you ask him for her hand in marriage? He's the closest thing she has to a father. I think Ben would like that."

"Thanks Ezra. I'll do that."

Elezar didn't so feel left out after talking to Ezra. Maybe this wedding thing wouldn't be so bad after all! He thought.

Abe walked in and Elezar rose to greet him.

"So, you are getting married?"

"Yes, how did you know?"

Abe just nodded toward the gathering of women. Freddie was in the middle of the din.

"Walk with me."

They left the compound and walked in the darkness.

"Abe, you have been my rock in these last days. I have discernment and power beyond my wildest dreams. I've grown in my Faith further than I ever thought possible. How can I ever thank you?"

"I was only the catalyst and the conduit. God saw in you what you didn't see in yourself, and yes, I would be honored to officiate at your wedding!"

Elezar was used to Abe's anticipation of his questions by now. He didn't yet know how but it seemed when they walked together their steps, their minds, and even their souls walked in syncopated time.

Elezar stopped suddenly and looked Abe in the eye, "You are no longer going to be my mentor?"

He didn't know where the knowledge came from. Abe's face lit up and a broad smile emerged.

"Ah, the pupil surpasses the teacher! You are correct. I can no longer take you higher in your walk with our Master. I must leave after your wedding to mentor another. We are going into the last days. All the souls that can be harvested soon will be. The second coming is near.

Elezar sensed the same.

"What do I do to prepare?"

"Listen to the Master, fast, and pray. You will have a pivotal role in the survival of the colony you have been charged with."

Elezar turned to face Abe to thank him but he was gone. Elezar turned to go back alone in the darkness. He was no longer afraid for he walked with the eternal light.

7

Family

Morning found the two betrothed back shouldering the responsibility of the colony. They left early as usual and resumed the familiar routine. Elezar kissed Freddie goodbye and walked into his job at the bread factory.

When Ben came in with a clean lab coat. Elezar asked him if he could walk as far as the safe house where Freddie was waiting. Ben smiled and agreed.

The day was routine and when his shift ended Elezar walked out as usual. About half-way to the house Ben caught up with him.

"Nice day for a stroll," said Ben, making small talk.

"Yes, it is!"

"They reached their destination. Freddie was waiting inside preparing for the trip. When she saw Ben, she ran to hug him. She hadn't seen him in a long time even though they were so close in proximity almost every day. They caught up on each other's lives for a few minutes until Freddie could hold her excitement no longer.

"Uncle, I'm getting married!"

"He couldn't help having a little fun at Elezar's expense.

"And who is the lucky guy?"

"Oh, Uncle you know!"

Elezar played along with the jest.

"We, uh I, thought it would be a nice gesture if this guy asked for her hand in marriage from the closest man she has to a father."

Freddie clutched her chest as tears welled in her eyes. Elezar had totally surprised her and Ben.

"Sir, I would like to ask you for your daughter's hand in marriage."

Ben was overwhelmed. He couldn't speak so he grabbed them both and hugged tight. Tears streamed down his cheeks. When he gained enough of his composure he answered with a resounding "YES!"

He pulled back and wiped his eyes, "When is the ceremony?"

Elezar shrugged, he didn't know.

"Next Friday at two-thirty," Freddie piped in.

It was Elezar's turn to be surprised.

"So soon?"

Yes, I didn't want to give you time to back out!" she teased.

"I would like to ask you something else, Uncle. Would you stand with me as a witness and my best man?"

"It would be an honor, Elezar. I wish my sister could see what a fine young man you have become!"

They both tried to hide their teary eyes with a hug.

"We must go, Elezar. It's getting dark," informed Freddie.

Ben hugged then both again and headed back to the factory. The two took their familiar path double time to race the sun home. The urgent fear was gone from their nightly tangos with time. Their God was always with them.

Thursday morning Ben brought in Elezar's fresh lab coat. Tomorrow was the big day and Ben was as excited as Elezar.

"Any butterflies?"

"No, none whatsoever; I couldn't imagine the rest of my life without her. I just wish I had more to give her."

Ben had a mischievous smile. He took a small box from his pocket and held it out for Elezar to see.

"I want you to have this."

"What is it?"

Elezar took the box and opened it. The diamonds in the wedding band sparkled in the light like brand new. He looked at his uncle in puzzled wonder. Before he could ask Ben spoke.

"I want you to have this. It belonged to your grandmother. Your grandfather gave it to her on their wedding day. It served them well. They were together until the end. Since I was the oldest it went to me when they passed. I never married but your father would not accept it from me because of his beliefs so my sister could wear it. I hope you will carry on the tradition."

Elezar was speechless. He gazed at the engagement and wedding ring. He vaguely remembered it on his grandmother's frail hand when she read to him as a child. He remembered how it sparkled when he moved it around on her finger.

"I...I don't know what to say!"

"Your eyes have said what I needed. Freddie and you will be married in a proper ceremony and given a ring that is worth more than the gold and diamonds it is made of. May your union be as fruitful as Jacob!

Elezar couldn't wait to give the engagement ring to Freddie at the end of the day. At least she would get to show it off for one day before the wedding. He could hardly contain his excitement when he saw her.

Finally, the day ended. Freddie was packing the bread for the trip across town.

Freddie and Elezar distributed the bread as usual. The day's fatigue settled in on Freddie. Along with the everyday commitments she was planning her big day. The terrible times they were in made a normal wedding impossible, but she was good at improvising.

When she finished, she turned to find Elezar standing with his right arm behind him. He had a radiant smile and a schoolboy excitement. He was too excited to be tired. He gingerly brought the ring box around for her to see. He opened the box to reveal the most beautiful ring she had ever seen!

"This was my grandmother's wedding ring. Her and my grandfather had many happy years together. Uncle Ben wanted us to have it," he explained.

She could only stare at the heirloom. Even in the dim light it shone with the eternal fire only a good diamond and true love can know.

He took the engagement ring out of its slot in the box and placed it on her finger. She admired the sparkle. The fit was perfect. She felt the love that it represented. She was speechless. She hugged Elezar, crying the happy tears of life that wash away hard times.

Curious onlookers made their way to the couple. Freddie snuck adoring looks of the ring behind Elezar's back when they embraced, as if it was going to vanish when she woke from her dream.

Sleep came late that night for both of them. Morning broke too early. At least today they would face a different challenge.

The women that were assisting the wedding preparations quarantined her in an upper floor of the high rise to transform Freddie the warrior into Frieda the beautiful bride. Elezar was not welcome.

When Freddie was safely out of sight he was taken to a different level and prepared. The men surrounded Elezar. Ezra spoke for the group.

"Since you and Frieda have been together, we have all prospered. We think you are a match made in Heaven. We want to give you something that will complete your union. Follow me."

The troupe led him to the upper level of the parking garage to an enclosed storage area. The outside looked ordinary, the same as it always looked. When Ezra opened the door Elezar couldn't believe his eyes. The inside had been transformed into a small one room apartment. The walls and floor were scrubbed clean. A double bed, neatly made, beckoned the weary with the promise of a good night's sleep. On the bed was a suite of clothes that seemed to be Elezar's size. They pushed him inside.

"Try on the clothes to see if they fit. Jed here has been working all week to get them ready in time."

A few minutes later Elezar appeared dressed for a wedding. Jed looked him up and down with a critical eye. He tugged the shoulders as he walked around the man. He flattened the lapel and stuck a few pins in the cuffs.

"Go take them off. I still have some work to do," Jed said as he showed him back into the room.

Elezar emerged with the clothes in hand and handed them to Jed. Ezra produced a chair and commanded Elezar to sit down. Immediately a barber's cloth was wrapped around his neck. Ezra began trimming his hair and beard.

Meanwhile, Freddy was on another level of the building enjoying a luxurious hot bath before getting the spa treatment, hair, nails, makeup. These resourceful people seemed to have all brought forth something for the wedding couple.

The preparations were winding down when Uncle Ben strolled in with several men from the compound. They brought the usual ration of bread and something extra. Some of the men gently deposited their burdens on the waiting table. They produced sheets and sheets of wedding cake lovingly baked by Ben.

The ones in charge of the banquet took over. With flowers grown on their own gardens and ribbons that were family treasures in these tough times they transformed the drab parking garage to a wonderful reception hall.

Ben was dressed in his finest. He was as nervous as the Bride and Groom. The time was drawing near. Abe quietly appeared like he always did, right on time.

The bridegroom took his place on the makeshift podium elevated so more could see. He smiled and nodded at Abe. The crowd was milling around, looking like the ripples on a sunlit lake. The singers brought the atmosphere to life and slowly, as his bride walked toward him the sea of people parted and there before him was the most beautiful queen he had ever seen. His Frieda had flowers woven in her hair like a halo on an angel. Her radiant smile brought him to the edge of tears. She walked arm in arm with Ben.

Ben gave away the bride and took his place beside Elezar for the ceremony. He thought about how much his sister would have liked to be there. Abe started the ceremony.

Elezar didn't remember much of the ceremony; he was too focused on Frieda. How did he deserve such a beautiful and loving wife? How was he going to provide for her? What did the future have in store for them? No matter what it was he would have her by his side. How could he ask for anything more?

He remembered saying "I DO!" and putting the ring on her finger and kissing the bride.

Frieda gazed into the eyes of the man she loved. She savored every word that Abe spoke as the ceremony unfolded. She knew whatever was in their future, they would face together. She knew this was a match made in heaven. She thought about her mother and father. How she wished they could be there. She was so grateful for Uncle Ben for giving her away. A few short months ago she was not sure this would ever happen to her.

"I now pronounce you husband and wife! You may kiss the bride."

Abe gave them time to embrace and turned them to the crowd.

"Good people of the Lord. I give you Mr. and Mrs. Elezar Aronivich!"

The crowd parted showing them the way to the reception. The wedding party traveled down the corridor of people greeting all as they made their way to the tables.

The whole colony had been working feverishly since the wedding announcement. The tables were moved from the abandoned mall. The chairs didn't match, and the table wear was a hodgepodge of everything they could scrounge but Frieda thought it was the most beautiful thing she had ever seen. The table was lined for the banquet with more food than she could ever imagine from the storehouse and the gardens. Ben's cake was the centerpiece.

When they got to their place of honor Ezra quieted the crowd.

"Today we are celebrating the union of two people who have given tirelessly to the well-being of us all; Elezar and Frieda Aronivich!"

He toasted the two newlyweds. The crowd burst into applause.

Elezar stood to address the crowd.

"I am the newest member of the colony, but I have a debt of gratitude to each and every one of you. You opened my eyes to the suffering that these hard times have inflicted on everyone. Without you I would be wondering the streets alone in the darkness of the world. Thank you all, and thank you Uncle for believing in me before I believed in myself!

Through the simple act of caring for others, I have been transformed."

He lifted his glass in tribute. The people did the same.

"Here is to my beautiful bride who brought me from a self-centered atheist to a Master in the Army of Christ!"

They all toasted and applauded loudly.

The crowd settled and Ben prayed.

"Lord, we give you thanks for allowing us to get together and celebrate with our family. We owe you everything! Please bless this union and the body of believers and keep us strong in the coming apocalyptic times. Bless this food that it will strengthen us physically that we may be able to bring more believers into your Kingdom."

The servers kept the bowls full of food that many of the small children had never tasted. Some of them had to be shown how to use a fork. They had never eaten anything they couldn't hold in their fingers.

Elezar looked down the table surveying the mothers and fathers using the special occasion to teach and nurture their children. He listened to the laughter; he watched the joyous interaction of the crowd. Tears welled in his eyes. This was life as it should be. He knew the next months would be treacherous, but he also knew who controlled their destiny. He squeezed Frieda's hand and kissed it.

It was time to cut the cake. They rose and Ben got the attention of the group. He handed Elezar a knife and he and Frieda cut the first piece together and enjoyed the first taste from each other's hand. They sat down and watched the reaction of the crowd. Most of the small children had never tasted anything like cake. Their eyes mirrored the ecstasy their tongues were experiencing.

Elezar smiled and seared the moment into his memory. The little children were, in awed silence, savoring every bite. Frieda and her new husband held hands and surveyed the joy their union caused. Elezar leaned in and kissed his new bride and kissed the back of her hand.

The banquet wound down, but the celebration didn't. Since most of the people came from a Jewish background the dancing and revelry went well into the night. The harsh reality of life was pushed aside.

When the crowd thinned Elezar whispered in Frieda's ear.

"I have a surprise for you! Follow me."

The remaining guests danced on, oblivious to the two guests of honor as they quietly left.

He led his new bride up the stairs to the place Ezra and his friends prepared for the newlyweds. When Elezar opened the door to the storage area, Frieda gasped. There was a real bed, decked out with a beautiful hand quilted bedspread, two real pillows with pillowcases, and a wardrobe for her meager clothes. She had a mirror hanging in front of a lavatory sporting a bouquet of flowers.   She cried. The people had sacrificed so much to make this a special day. She turned to Elezar and wept in his arms. He was a little puzzled by the tears but relished any time his wife turned to him for strength and support.

8

The Beast

Truth is fiction and fiction truth. The Beast from the sea controlled the warp. The ones loyal to the New World Order, The Realm, believed what they had to to get the next day's supply of the Amy. Just when the enemy, Christians and Jews, were thought to be eradicated, a new colony would be discovered, and the troopers called to war.

The aftermath of the battles was shown on the state-controlled TV. Even the dullest of the subjects questioned (only in their mind, of course) the reports. The "victories" of the Realm, although given different names and places, looked remarkably the same and the Enemy looked remarkably like fellow subjects. But eventually, what used to disturb the mind's slumber was accepted as the norm.

The Trilateral and Mr. Rothfella seemed to get more powerful day by day. Every missile, every laser rifle, every truck and tank were supplied by the Trilateral. Every ounce of the Amy was provided by them. All wealth moved through their bank. Those given to conspiracy theories accused them of marking law abiding, loyal, New World Order subjects with Christian heresy, just to profit from the carnage. Rumors circulated about whole colonies of the Realm disappearing overnight, never to be heard from again.

"Collateral damage," they were called.

The accused disappeared behind bars to await a trial by the tribunal. They usually never made it to trial. POLICY OF THE REALM; Amy was withheld from anyone incarcerated. By the second day of forced abstinence, the madness caused the accused to tear at their own flesh until they died.

This was condoned by the Beast, or just ignored—same outcome. Due process didn't exist in this New World Order. The Beast didn't care. He was wrapped up in his own misery from the assassination attempt. He didn't care about anything, except the next pill to ease the pain.

He often lamented about what could have been if the Christians hadn't destroyed half of his brain. He sometimes wished that he hadn't survived, but then he could never die, he knew that. The words he read as a child in the last book of the Bible told of the triumph of the God of Abraham, but he felt the power in his youthful invincibility of another god, his father, Satan. He shuddered at the realization that he was doomed to torment for a thousand years along with his father. He dares not think that thought.

He wanted to destroy most of these retched humans with their own nuclear weapons. It would simplify his life. They were so needy. He just wanted enough of them to survive to serve him. Father Satan had other ideas. He knew that the only real power he had against The Creator was the misery he inflicted on His children.

Why would an all-powerful Creator give these retched beings free will to choose their own destiny? It was so easy to tempt them and turn them to evil. The capacity for evil existed within each and every one of them; his father Satan used their dark side for his pleasure...

Nicholas' thoughts were interrupted by the presence of pure evil.

"We have implemented animal sacrifice again in the Temple, only now the god they are sacrificing to is me!"

"That is excellent, my Lord." Nicholas said, trying to sound engaged, "But you haven't stilled the voices of the Prophets in the square. I hear them day and night! No matter what I do their voice echoes in my brain. It is driving me insane!"

He felt his throat tighten as he was lifted off his throne by his neck. No hand was visible, but Nicholas knew the presence's power.

"The Beast brought forth on the land, the Deceiver, will prevail; it is just a matter of time. He is preaching the need for human sacrifices now to ensure their lives are not interrupted by any more of the plagues of Egypt."

Satan did not have control of that. How could he promise such a thing? thought Nicholas.

Even the thought of human sacrifice to his golden image in the Temple did little to engage Nicholas. He couldn't wait until the evil presence left him alone in his own misery.

Satan was still furious about being banished to earth. His failed efforts to destroy the nation of Israel, God's chosen people and especially the one called Jesus, still angered him. He would get revenge.

It came to him as he was toying with Nicholas. He released his son and let him fall back on the throne he was sitting on. Just as the God had taken the first born from The Egyptians when he brought the Israelites out of slavery, he would take the firstborn of Israel now.

The smell of hot sulfur was heavy in the room. He turned his attention again to his son.

"I want you to call together the troopers patrolling all of Israel. Command them to capture all the unmarked women they can find that are well along in their first pregnancy. When the time is right, we will have a sacrificial ceremony like the world has never see! The women must be beautiful. The one we pick for the honor must be flawless."

When the prince of darkness left his presence, Nicholas summoned his faithful assistant Chione.

She would take care of the details for him. She was the most loyal of the entire demon possessed. She raised him from a toddler. She would know the ones to call on the hunt.

She entered his chambers fifteen minutes later, not wanting to keep Nicholas waiting. She had felt the sting of his demented, drug and pain induced anger. He once killed his security officer for bringing him bad news.

"You called?"

He was rubbing his forehead and temples trying to massage away the constant pain.

"I was just honored with a visit from my father. He has requested that we find all the women with no mark that are pregnant with their firstborn. The one he chooses will be ceremonially sacrificed in the temple. Offer a million bitcoin and a year's supply of Amy. That should get the interest of all the bounty hunters."

"One other thing; If one hair of the women is disturbed, they will answer to me personally, are we clear? I will not have a sacrifice that is damaged in any way!"

"Yes, Master I will see to this immediately. This may take a long time. Most of the unmarked have been accounted for and eliminated."

"Not my problem, just get it done."

She bowed and left the room. Nicholas had always known Chione. He trusted her loyalty, but he also knew she was intricately connected to His father and confided everything to him. He watched his attitude around her now more than ever.

Chione always breathed a sigh of relief when she left his presence. She saw what he did to his loyal head of security just for suggesting he rethink his position on nuclear holocaust. She had to summon his father Satan and put a stop to his madness.

Since Satan ruled the Realm through his son and the Deceiver the One World Order had stabilized. The loyal marked citizens were compliant as sheep. The Realm condoned all forms of wickedness, degradation, and immoral conduct as long as they supported the Realm politically.

9

The Sacrifice

The newlyweds returned to their daily routine. The colony still needed the bread. The gardens were flourishing, and the bartering brought in the needed proteins, although barely enough.

Elezar led the daily expeditions now. His faith increased daily. He was able to sense danger and use his gift to insure safe passage to and from the bread factory. The colony seemed to grow daily. The Prophets were opening the eyes and hearts of the Jews to the Way.

Of course, this put more burden on the newlyweds to provide enough bread. Elezar lamented that the portions seemed to be getting smaller every day.

When the two of them were alone in their apartment, Elezar sat on the edge of the bed and buried his face in his hands.

"What are we going to do Freddie? This isn't working, we're not keeping pace with the demand."

"Why don't you talk to your uncle about getting more? I'm sure he would be willing if we could find a safe way to move it."

She took his hands and pulled his arms around her. She had that look in her eyes. Elezar's worries dissipated as she kissed him. They were oblivious to the whole world as they came together.

A few hours of blissful sleep later Elezar woke with a start. A big smile creased his face. It was so simple! God had given him the means to move as much bread as they needed. Excited, he woke Freddie.

"Have we got any more duffel bags?" he asked.

Freddie was not fully awake. She rolled over face to face with him.

"What does that have to do with anything?"

"The Lord has given me the solution to our supply problem. I have to talk to Uncle Ben, but I think he'll be all for my plan."

"That's not how you wake up a new bride!"

He smiled, "And just how do you wake a new bride?"

"Come here and let me show you."

The morning would just have to wait!

· · ·

They hurriedly put on their clothes and came together for one last kiss before they opened the door to the rest of the world. Elezar would be late for work if they didn't hurry. While Freddie was getting ready

Elezar hurried down the stairs. People were already milling around preparing to meet the challenges of the day. He spotted Greta.

"Greta, Can I have a word with you?"

She approached him smiling, "What can I help you with?"

"I need two more duffels and two able bodied men to help transport more bread today. I'm going to ask Ben If I can change the way we smuggle it out and how much he can spare."

The possibility of more sustenance for the group piqued her interest. She knew who to ask to go with them. Ezra and Ted were "voluntold." They didn't mind, they were also part of a small group that went out every day and scrounged for food or took goods the colony produced and bartered for necessities.

Freddie came down the stairs ready to go. When the two men grabbed the two extra duffels and followed Elezar and her out the entrance she was puzzled.

"Why are they coming along?"

"I'm taking a leap of faith today. I'm going to ask Ben if we can have more of the bread. I had a revelation last night. I'm not using my talents nearly enough to be proficient. Someday, I may be called on to do something I'm not yet qualified for. I need practice working on God's time and with Ben's help we will all benefit."

She wasn't sure what he meant but she would go on faith until she understood.

When they got to the safe house, Freddie and the two men stayed behind and Elezar went to work as usual. When he got settled into his routine Ben came in and handed Elezar his fresh lab coat.

"Uncle, can I talk to you about the bread?"

"Of course, Elezar, what do you need to know?"

"It occurred to me I wasn't using the skills God gave me to the fullest. I haven't been in a situation where I have had to use it for a while. I wonder if it is something I need to work on like any craft to be good."

"What are you getting at, nephew?"

"Can you produce more bread than you do now without getting caught?"

"Of course! I'm usually only producing at fifty percent capacity. I'm usually waiting on qualified workers. I can't find anyone dependable for the mixing lines."

"Uncle! I have two people with me today that can learn. They would be the best employees you've ever had, next to me of course!"

Ben shook his head in false embarrassment at Elezar's tongue-in- cheek boasts.

"I'm sure you do and I'm sure none of them have the mark. I'm taking a big chance having you around, let alone two more undocumented people to sneak past the guards every day."

"You took the training and know the Way. You know that the power of God is limited only by our doubts and fears. I want to step out in faith and grow in the power that God has given me."

"What do you have in mind nephew?"

"I want to be able to move freely like Abe does. If I can get the men in here, will you train them?"

"Of course. But how are you going to get the product out of here unnoticed?"

"I haven't thought that far ahead." If I'm successful getting the men in and out God will show me the way."

Ben was impressed with Elezar's faith and willingness to grow. This was a dangerous undertaking, but Ben felt that God wanted him to help. A silent intuition told him that Elezar would face many trials in the months ahead. They both needed to be ready.

I'll be praying for you. Get the men in here and I'll mentor them for as long as I have to."

Elezar decided to exit the security gate without using his wrist pass just to see if he could. The guard confronted him as he left. Elezar moved his time wave slightly so the guard couldn't see him but when he tried to get through the gate it was locked!

He raised his other hand and moved the wave until he heard the mechanism click. He hurried past the gate. When it closed, he noticed the guard waving his gun around in the air at the nothingness in front of him. Elezar smiled.

He hurried back to the safe house.

"Ezra, Ted, I have a new job for you if you are interested."

They both looked skeptically at him. No mark, no jobs, they knew that but weren't sure Elezar did.

"Sure, what are we going to do, make bread?" Ezra said his voice dripping sarcasm.

"As a matter of fact, yes!"

They both snickered at Elezar thinking he was joking.

"All we have to do is get you past security and Uncle Ben will train you."

They looked at each other realizing that he wasn't joking.

"How are we going to get through the gate?" asked Ted.

"We could shoot our way in once." Ezra chimed in.

"I can get you in and out safely if you have enough faith."

Elezar said it forcefully, confidently, sounding almost cocky.

They thought about the bounty of extra bread. They thought about Elezar and Freddie and how they risked their lives daily to feed the people. They looked at each other mirroring their decision.

"Ok, hotshot, how do you propose that we get in?" asked Ezra.

"You have to do exactly what I say when I say it. We will confront the gatekeeper together. When he comes out to investigate, I'll move us through the gate so he can't see us."

"How are you going to do that?" Ezra asked.

"I will use the power Abe taught me to get out undetected. I don't know how to explain it to you, but I have faith that at the right time God will provide."

They knew God's power, they knew Elezar's faith, and they knew the needs of the colony.

"OK." They said in unison.

Elezar kissed his bride and nodded toward the door. When they approached the gatehouse, he motioned the two to align behind him.

Elezar raised his hand until he heard the gate unlock. The three of them moved in unison into the factory. When the gatekeeper heard the latch, he moved into the walkway to block anyone from entering. He saw three shadowy figures, one behind the other for a fleeting moment but they seemed to vanish into thin air.

This is the second time today I've seen ghosts. The gatekeeper thought to himself. He took another hit on the bottle of Amy he had stashed under his desk.

Ezra and Ted followed Elezar into the factory. People were milling around getting ready for their daily routine. Some were loafing, some were talking, and some were working. They all ignored the presence of the three as they made their way into the place that was to be Ted and Ezra's workstation.

When they were safely inside Elezar lowered his hand and his head. Until that point, he was unaware how much personal energy he had to expend to bend time. He put his hand on his knees for a minute to recover his composure. Ezra and Ted could only stare in wide eyed amazement.

Ben entered the room with two lab coats. He was wearing one himself.

They nodded greetings to each other.

"Are you men ready to learn the fine art of baking the best bread in the world?"

They both just nodded but deep down they were overcome with thanksgiving at the wonder of their God. They both refused the mark to follow the Lord and were convinced that they would never hold a job again. It was a price they were willing to pay.

They eagerly followed Ben with their new clip-boards for taking notes in their pristine white lab coats.

Elezar made his way to his workstation. He anticipated more bread coming down the line than usual and prepared for it. He brought one of the duffels with him. He had an interim plan to get more bread out. Before his first break, he not only filled his lab coat, but he also filled the duffel. He strapped the duffel on his back and boldly walked out into the yard. He was careful to keep his time wave just enough ahead to thwart the guards.

The gate swung open for another employee, and he sauntered out unseen. He stayed just out of sync until he entered the house. Freddie gasped when he suddenly appeared in the doorway. She usually could see his progress down the sidewalk. Her eyes opened wide when he brought the already full duffel around and sat it in front of her. He took off his coat and emptied the pockets.

"I need another duffel bag."

Freddie grabbed one she had hidden. He kissed her goodbye for a little while and headed back to work. He stayed out of sync until he reached the gate. No one was there so he moved the waves until he found a time when the gate was open and walked in. He was learning how to manipulate the time waves just like a harpist learns the subtleties of the harp to control beautiful musical waves.

Back at his post the mundane was welcomed. His escapades into time left him drained, but he was young and recovered quickly. He "tested" more bread than usual so he could fill the backpack and the lab coat, just as before. By the time he was done the lunch bell rang. Once again, he made his way to the safe house loaded down with bread. He wondered how the two new hires were getting along.

"The key to wonderful bread is letting the yeast work. If you hurry the yeast, the rest is a waste. Mix the ingredients thoroughly. Don't rush the batch of dough, let it breath."

Ezra rolled his eyes at the number of times Ben had said that in the course of the morning. He and Ted were wondering when they would be able to make some bread on their own. The lunch bell rang, and Ben led them to the break room to enjoy the bread they would be making. Ted and Ezra agreed there was no bread on earth that tasted as good as

Ben's. They understood his passion but wondered when they would get their chance.

At lunch Ben and the two new hires talked and laughed and got to know each other. The bell rang and Ben got up abruptly and looked at his watch.

"Well, men, I have a meeting in fifteen minutes. I think I've tortured you enough for one day. Go make me some bread!"

The two were beaming. They were going to get their chance. They walked back to work in silence going over what Ben had drilled into them the whole morning. They wouldn't admit it but they both had butterflies when they walked through the workstation doors.

Ted grabbed his clipboard and read the first notes out loud. Ezra walked to the various stations to push the buttons that brought all the ingredients down into the mixing vat. Each had to be added in the proper order and mixed for a preset time. In a few minutes the gigantic mixing vat was churning with the bread dough. Their first batch! They tested the density of the dough and the texture like Ben had instructed, only twice as much. They wanted to make sure they got it right! The big machine finally dumped the mass into another machine that metered the dough into small portions in the moving pans.

They watched the little dabs of dough rise in the warming ovens until it nearly overflowed the bread pans. The yeast was working. They watched their first batch disappear into the oven. They both were grinning from ear to ear. There was something deeply satisfying about working, especially when it was for the good of the whole colony. The bread would taste sweeter tonight at the dinner table knowing they helped create it.

The day ended. Elezar popped in the door.

"Ready!"

"Just a minute, we have to finish our checklist so we will be ready in the morning," replied Ted."

Elezar waited patiently for them to finish, after all what are a few minutes in the waves of time!

When they fell in line to leave, he could see the thank you in their eyes. What a day they had!

He stopped by his lab and grabbed the duffel full of bread. Single file they started on their journey. Just like on the way in, Elezar kept the wave slightly different. There were many people exiting, so they walked through the opened gate.

When they got to the door of the house, Elezar tried to move the time wave to a time when the door was open. He miscalculated and hit nose first into the door followed by Ezra and Ted.

Freddie heard the commotion and opened the door. There was Elezar bent over with his fingers gingerly feeling his nose. The two men with him recovered enough to start laughing at their situation.

"Why didn't you just turn the knob or knock?" Freddie asked before she burst out in laughter.

Ezra and Ted followed Elezar into the house. Elezar paced the floor still holding his nose. When he walked by the door, he slammed it. The trio were trying hard to stifle their laughs and were succeeding until Elezar, convinced that his nose wasn't broken or bleeding, started to giggle at the absurdity of his plight. They all had a big laugh at the time traveler's expense.

They had to get down to business. They had bread to deliver. The four duffels were packed with bread, and they were ready to go. Freddie took point and Elezar brought up the rear.

Elezar didn't let on to the others but his nose plant on the door shook his confidence. He was getting cocky and careless. The gift he had should not be used frivolously. Maybe God just tweaked his nose to warn him, he thought. He still had a lot to learn!

The four of them settled into a routine. The bread was so plentiful now that rationing wasn't necessary. They had some left for other meals now.

The tables that were assembled for the wedding served as dining tables now. The bounty of the crops and the bartering provided enough food that the people prepared dishes and enjoyed family dining again. The youngest children had never experienced actual cooked meals and had to be taught table manners.

Elezar marveled at how far the colony had come with the help of God! The Realm did their best to control every aspect of everyone's life, but they couldn't control love.

10

End Times

E lezar wasn't feeling well when he woke. The welts raised all over his body. Freddie was the same. He heard the painful crying of little children in the colony. When they investigated, everyone in the colony had raised welts.

"Should we go to work today or stay home and try to help?" Elezar asked Freddie.

"I don't know what we can do here. Boils are part of the plagues that will come. We need to make sure they are fed and cared for. The boils will pass in time."

Elezar and the crew left as usual for work. The trip seemed to become more painful the longer they traveled. Ted and Ezra felt feverish and weak. The two young newlyweds fared better but movement was becoming more painful. Freddie regretted the decision to carry on as usual. She could see now that it was going to take perseverance just to make it back home.

The three men approached the gate. Elezar got them through safely. Inside, the factory seemed almost empty. Very few workers braved the pain to make bread. The three moved quickly to their workstations. Ben came in to greet Ezra and Ted. They saw the red sores on him and saw the pain in his eyes.

He greeted them cheerfully and handed them their lab coats. He was determined to not let a few welts take his joy. They took the lab coats and got down to business. They could sense he was in no mood for small talk.

Ben made his way to Elezar's workstation. Ben noticed the painful sores on Elezar.

"How are you doing today?"

"Not good. Freddie and all the people in the colony have these painful sore spots that seem to be getting worse. Let me tell you Uncle, it was a chore just to get here today."

"I'm grateful you came. Ted and Ezra may be the only ones making bread today. Not very many showed for work. I can't blame them. Every time I move it is painful!"

Elezar was preoccupied scratching his arms.

"Do you think Abe would help us?"

Ben smiled that knowing smile that drove Elezar crazy.

"I'm sure he can, but maybe he's not the one God chose."

"What do you mean by that?"

"I have never seen anyone possess the incredible gift you have. You can heal these people in time."

Elezar pondered what Ben said. *In time, of course, I can move them to a place in the future when the boils will be gone!*

"But I have never gone more than a few minutes in time. What if I can't do this?"

"With God all things are possible. Ask for strength and wisdom. If it is his will, you will be enabled."

"If I take them into the future, will I have to leave them there? What happens if I can go to the future when the sickness has run its course and then bring them back? Will the boils return? What consequences will we all face if I alter time in this way?"

Elezar was thinking out loud.

"Only God has the answers you seek."

Elezar remembered his training. He thought, *I'd been gone a day, but it was actually a week. I felt no ill effects from the experience. Maybe the restrictions man's knowledge put on time didn't apply. The only way to know is to pray and step out in faith.*

Elezar dropped to his knees and asked for enlightenment and strength. He didn't know how long he prayed but when he rose a wave of calm swept over him.

"Ben, will you go with me. I want to try to heal you and me. I'll take us as far as it takes to see the boils disappear. I'll bring us back and see if we get them again."

Ben nodded. Elezar said a prayer and raised his hand. He groaned as he shoved the invisible barrier with all his might. He wasn't sure if his body actually moved or not. He and Ben were adrift in a different world. A tranquil world with a divine presence that defied their feeble attempts to discern what was happening. They returned to human consciousness staggering from the forces they felt.

When Elezar focused his eyes, Ben was standing in the same spot. Elezar checked his sores. They were gone! Ben took his shirt off to check some of the lesions on his body. They were gone!

They looked at each other and said in unison, "God's time!"

Elezar looked at the clock on the wall. It hadn't moved!

"I have to go to Ezra and Ted and see if I can do the same thing for them!"

Ben was in total agreement. He was still in awe.

"I feel like I've seen what heaven is like!"

Elezar hoped he could have the same experience with the two bread makers. He burst into their workstation elated.

"If you are willing, I can heal you."

Men in misery will listen to someone offering hope, even if it means they have to stretch their faith.

"What do we have to do?" asked Ezra.

"Just believe."

Elezar positioned himself in front of them and prayed. He raised his hand and with all his being brought them into a new world. One that had no time as man knows time—God's time. He felt the familiar, all-encompassing power of the Creator. When the trio came back to the world, they were in the same place they left. Ted and Ezra checked themselves for the boils. There were none! The pain and the scars were completely gone. They fell to their knees and worshipped.

"I have to get to Freddie and heal her and the rest of the colony. You two and Ben will have to get the rest of the bread we need tonight. I'm going to show the rest of the people what God's healing power is really like!"

"Go!" they said in unison.

Elezar ran out of the gate. This time he knocked when he got to the safe house door. Freddie was in so much pain she was slow to get to the door and unlock it. Elezar's exuberance made her groan in agony. She turned away from him and slowly made her way to the place she was sitting. She just wanted him to go away and let her suffer. He tried to show her his arms, but it didn't register that he was free of boils. He stripped to his bare chest.

"No boils!"

"She looked at him in disbelief. How could that be? She thought.

She touched his arm and ran her fingers down his chest and looked at him puzzled.

"Come with me and be healed."

He took her hand and raised his palm. The veil lifted and they were suspended in God's time; It always was, it always is, and it always will be! She felt the all-encompassing love and the pain vanished. In an instant they were standing where their journey started!

She touched her arms. All the pain was gone. The incessant itching and scars had vanished! She fell to her knees in prayer along with Elezar.

"We have to get to the colony!" she said.

"I know."

Elezar thought for a minute.

"What if I lift the veil and take us to yesterday when we walked through the entrance to the colony?"

He took her hand and concentrated on the time and place. He raised his hand and the waves warped slightly. Instantly they were home.

They walked into the stench of disease and the moaning of the infirmed. Freddie cried when she saw the suffering. Elezar took charge.

"Is there anyone that has left the compound to barter or hunt?"

Greta shook her head no, "We are all here."

"I need you to focus on what I say! God can stop the misery. All he asks is that you have faith! Please gather together in the banquet hall.

When they were assembled and quiet, Elezar raised both palms and shoved for all his might. The veil moved and engulfed the mass of humanity. When they were again back in the compound the whole multitude was healed of their afflictions.

They were jumping and shouting and praising God! They didn't notice at first that Elezar was lying unconscious on the floor. They immediately took him to his bed. Freddie fussed over him. Praying under her breath for his recovery.

The thought crossed her mind, who will heal the physician?

He woke weakly to her loving touch.

"I'll be alright. When that much energy passes through it takes time to recover. He kissed her hand and fell into a deep sleep.

His body seemed to float. He moved effortlessly to the to the sea. The water lapped at his feet peacefully as he walked along the shore. He looked toward the reddish sunset rays dancing on the water. The rays deepened in color and raced to shore. He looked down at blood-red water swelling with the tide. He was swept away to a peaceful babbling stream. When the sun rose over the trees the vibrant stream flowed blood red.

The sun's scorching noonday rays burned the grass along the bank of the river. He fled to a large tree for shade. The leaves withered and the sun's anger burned his shoulders and seared his eyes blind. Darkness enveloped the earth.

He was transported to the square. He smiled at the thought of hearing the prophets again, but the square was silent. He woke shivering.

11

Life Renewed

Elezar told the colony of his dreams. Some of the elders gathered around him to pray. They recognized Revelation but wondered why he had been spared the last and final bowl? Life's struggles resumed for the newlyweds.

They left every morning only to return in the evening burdened with as much bread as they and the two bread makers could carry. Weeks passed. The marked were still struggling with the sores. The troopers on patrol were still in misery so it was easier to slip by, even without using Elezar's gift.

One morning the group left as usual, Elezar was on point with Freddie next and Ezra and Ted bringing up the rear. For no apparent reason, Freddie broke away. It was out of character for her to leave unannounced.

"Elezar! Wait a minute, Freddie's gone!"

Ezra pointed in the direction she went.

"You guys stay here, and I'll go look for her.

Ted and Ezra were both fathers. They looked at each other and grinned. They knew.

When Elezar found her, she was bent over, trying her best to hold her flowing hair back, wiping her mouth on her sleeve. She looked peaked. Elezar spied her handiwork on the ground and got a little woozy himself.

"What's the matter, babe?"

"I missed my last period and now I have morning sickness. I think I'm pregnant!"

"But how?"

She rolled her eyes; men could be such morons sometimes! She was in no mood to explain the birds and the bees.

"I mean I know how this happened, but I wasn't prepared for..."

"YOU weren't prepared!"

Elezar knew words weren't going to help, especially his yammering. He did the only thing he could. He pulled her close and just held her gently. She sobbed softly in his arms until the nausea passed. She rested her head on his arm, grateful for his strength. The feeling passed finally, and she looked up at him. His eyes were in a far-off place, no doubt contemplating this life changing event, so she pulled his beard and got his attention.

She smiled, he smiled, he picked her off the ground and twirled her around, his eyes dancing. They were going to have a baby!

"I think I'd better stay here today; I don't want to slow you down."

"OK, let's go back to the colony and announce the news!"

They went back toward Ezra and Ted. Elezar motioned them back to the compound. The morning meal was in full swing when they arrived. Morning smells that tweaked the appetite of everyone else brought the nausea back for Freddie. She smiled weakly at the cheering crowd as Elezar broke the exciting news. The men were pounding him on the back and shaking his hand.

She just wanted to slink away to her bed and sleep. Greta and some of the other women rescued her. They whisked her away from the testosterone two-step going on in the banquet hall and made sure she was comfortable.

Ezra saw his fourteen -year-old son standing off from the crowd. He was a good son, but their relationship was strained lately. Ezra thought of the time he got the news that Elezar just received. He still remembered the elation. He was holding on too tight to Timothy. He knew it but in these hard times it was tough to let go. Timothy stayed behind and tended the garden spot his father started when they came here, but he longed to get out in the world and see the things his father saw. Ezra pulled Elezar to the side.

"We're going to be shorthanded today. Would it be possible for my son Timothy to go with us? We don't get to do much together and this is the perfect opportunity to let him experience the outside world."

Elezar didn't hesitate. He thought about his own father. He only had the memories now. How could he stand in the way of their memories?

"Yes, bring him! We could use his strong back."

Elezar watched Timothy's eyes light up when he got the news he was going on an adventure with his father.

The small troupe left again for the bakery. When they arrived, Ben was already preparing the first batch. Most of his entire workforce was gone now. The sores and the effects of the Amy left them with little ambition to work. He was at least going to get enough made for the colony, and he wanted to get the shipment to the palace of the Beast so his bakery wouldn't lose its preferred status.

"Who is our newest recruit?" Ben asked when he saw Timothy.

"This is my son, Timothy. Timothy, meet Benjamin Ben-Hadid. Ben is the owner of this bread factory. He is the man responsible for the bread you eat every day!" explained Ezra.

Ben extended his hand in greeting like he would to a peer. Timothy took it proudly, flattered to be treated as an adult.

"'Would you like to tour the factory, Timothy?"

His eyes opened wide. "Yes, I'd like that."

"We'll have to get you a proper lab coat." Ben said as he handed the two workers theirs.

"I have one more stop at the quality control lab to see Elezar and we'll tour."

Timothy glanced at his father for approval. Ezra nodded.

"I'll bring him back in about two hours after the tour."

"Mind your manners and listen to Ben."

"I will father."

Ben entered Elezar's lab followed by Timothy, brimming with importance in his new white lab coat.

"I see you've met Timothy."

"Yes, a fine young man and future bread maker."

Timothy beamed.

"Yes, he is filling in temporarily for Freddie."

Ben's demeanor changed. "What's wrong with Freddie?"

"She's feeling a little under the weather today."

Elezar did his best to be serious and tweak Ben, but he couldn't hide his excitement.

"Morning sickness," Elezar said, "We're going to have a baby!"

Ben hugged Elezar, then slapped him on the back.

"Freddie is the one I should be hugging; she'll do all the work!"

"She'll be back after she gets over the morning sickness. Meanwhile, Timothy can fill in."

"Yes, we're going to tour the factory and then he is going to learn bread making from his father."

Elezar smiled at the duo as they left and turned his attention to work. It was hard for him to concentrate. He kept thinking of Freddie and daydreaming of his new life.

Elezar couldn't wait for the day to end so he could get home to Freddie. Since she wasn't there to organize and pack all the bread, he enlisted Timothy. When the whistle blew Elezar checked Timothy's handiwork. There were four duffels neatly packed by the door ready for transport.

When the two bread makers came in, Elezar motioned behind the door and grabbed the nearest one, adjusting it on the way. Timothy struggled so Ezra helped him get the pack situated. The other two followed with their bags.

"Stay in line behind Elezar." Ezra barked at Timothy.

Ted brought up the rear, always on the lookout. They made their way through the factory to the exit. Elezar had already warped the time wave. All he had to do now was make sure the gate was open when they reached it. The fiasco with the door to the safe house was always in the back of his mind. He breathed a sigh of relief when they were safely through. A few blocks down, in an alley he stopped and normalized the wave. Around them, the air resembled a mirage in the dessert until everything stabilized.

They didn't stick around long. Elezar had to get back to Freddie. The rest of the trip was routine.

Elezar burst into the doorway scanning the faces for his Freddie. He spotted her sitting with a group of women.

"You're late!" she chided

"Are you OK?"

"Of course, almost every woman goes through the sickness when they get pregnant."

She rose to give him a kiss. His anxiety faded with the touch of her lips. She walked over to help him distribute the bread.

"Should you be doing that in your condition?" He asked, following her.

She stopped suddenly and he ran in to her.

"I'll be fine, don't be so overprotective!" she said, pushing him away.

He walked behind her like a pit bull protecting its master.

A few days later Freddie resumed her duties beside Elezar, but instead of going to the safe house, she came into the factory with the rest of them. Elezar was getting proficient at moving the group through the time waves safely and felt at ease bringing them all in as a group.

They had decided to keep Timothy on the team when she returned. The extra bread brought a good price in the marketplace barter. The storage areas were full. The colony that was on the verge of starvation a few months ago now had plenty to eat.

12

Red Life, Red Death

The sores began to heal on the marked. Life was beginning to get back to normal. The factory was once again producing enough bread to meet the demand. The Deceiver blamed the disease on the people. They were not loyal enough. They didn't worship Satan with total commitment. The animal sacrifices in the temple seemed to coincide with the end to the sores, or so the news media reported. No one was ready for what came next.

No one knew the origin of the blood. It seemed to boil out of the sea from an invisible volcano. The tentacles of red reached the shores of every ocean on the planet. The sea life died at an alarming rate and washed to shore. The blood coagulated in their gills, and they suffocated. Every kind of creature, big and small, rotted on the beaches. The stench worked its way inland on the ocean breezes, another insidious demon tormenting the marked day and night.

Many of the large ships were lost to the demonic madness. The stench and the blood were everywhere. The salt air lifted it and broadcast it. The waves painted it on the decks of the ships, and it would not be removed.

When the ocean carnage subsided, the blood appeared in the rivers and streams. The city water treatment plants were overwhelmed. The supply of Amy was disrupted. There simply was not enough untainted water. The Amy went to the highest bidder. The rest were left to their madness. Mutilated corpses littered the streets. The colony had to suspend all operations for their own safety.

Elezar called all the people in the colony together.

"We will ration what bread we have left until we can safely leave the compound. Ezra, Ted, Timothy, you will be in charge of the distribution. Please don't leave the compound for any reason. The Elders and I have conferred and agree that it is not safe for any travel or bartering."

There was grumbling throughout the compound, but they knew he spoke the truth. Everyone brought what they had to share. They would get through this together. Someone was at the well praying, day and night, thanking God for the clean water.

Elezar requested a private meeting with the Elders. Freddie was at his side.

"I fear for Ben's life. I would like your blessing and prayers to go tomorrow at first light to bring him into the colony until this passes."

They nodded and conferred for a few minutes before giving him their blessing.

When they were alone Freddie begged to go with Elezar. Up until the last week she had accompanied them to the bread factory, but she had to stop. She was six months along now and struggled with the weight of the duffel full of bread.

She was already restless. She had always been in control of her own destiny. Now she had a husband and a new life inside her to consider when she made her choices. She wished some days Elezar would whisk them back and forth in the time waves, but he used his ability wisely.

He looked into her pleading eyes and couldn't say no. He knew there was always risk, but he missed being with her. It seemed that the demands of the colony and the daily bread runs kept them apart. She loved Ben as much as he did. They were both so grateful for what he did to ensure the survival of the colony.

"We will go in the morning at first light before the workers show."

Her elation was short lived. Her baby sensed her joy and started stretching and kicking inside her. She doubled slightly and took Elezar's hand and placed it on her belly. He froze with wonder as the two little feet stretched and distorted her abdomen.

Their eyes locked in the wondrous moment in time that bonds two people with the wonder of the life they created. They spent the night in each other's arms planning the future, knowing full well the future was not theirs to plan. No matter, they were together.

Morning broke and the two moved quietly to the exit. Elezar felt a strange phenomenon when he passed through the entrance. Something like the sensation of time travel. He was too excited to think much of it. This was like old times for the two newlyweds.

Freddie got directly behind him just as he raised his hands and shoved. They were inside the factory in Elezar's lab instantly. The factory seemed deserted when they opened the door. Elezar, with Freddie right behind, made their way to the third-floor office/residence of Uncle Ben.

"I don't have a good feeling about this!" he whispered to Freddie.

He heard loud, angry voices inside Ben's office when they approached. Elezar squeezed Freddie's hand to let her know he was going to warp. The door burst open and a trooper in full gear burst out. By the look on the trooper's face, uncle Ben was in real trouble. Elezar moved them through the door. On the inside Ben was bound to a chair and the Sargent was in his face.

Ben was calm water to their tidal waves.

"Why did you stop bread production!" the angry man spit at Ben.

"I have already explained to your trooper that I refuse to make bread with tainted water. At the present time there is no clean water in this section of Jerusalem."

"The Beast demands his bread. If you can't produce it then I will have to replace you and let the Beast know you don't have the mark! Rumor has it that not all the bread produced here gets to the trucks, a clear violation of the agreement you made to produce the bread in exchange for your freedom."

"All bread except the quality control loaves make their way to the trucks," Ben stated calmly.

He was getting a little worried. He talked to these men on a regular basis. They all seemed to be reasonable men. The difference now was they were on half rations of the Amy and were very excitable. He had already explained as calmly as he could why he wasn't making bread. They couldn't grasp any of his reasoning in their slow slip into the Amy madness. The trooper that left the room went to retrieve a vial of truth serum the Army of the Realm used to extract information from prisoners.

Ben was afraid that he would betray the colony when they used it on him. He prayed earnestly for God to not let that happen.

Elezar and Freddie were now behind Ben. The Troopers were in a half circle around him, waiting on the truth serum to arrive.

"Grab my knife!"

Freddie didn't hesitate. She didn't know what he had in mind, but she would be ready.

Elezar gave a shove and the time wave warped like the pleat on a curtain, engulfing Ben.

The platoon was distracted by the arrival of the truth serum and didn't notice their prey was gone. Freddie sawed frantically at Ben's bindings while Elezar held them in time.

When he was free, Elezar shoved and they were in the safe house they used to get the bread distributed. Elezar had to rest. The precision that he used to warp the wave took a lot of energy. He was exhausted and had to get his bearings. Ben peered out the door facing the factory.

"I'm sure glad you showed when you did! I was praying for deliverance but had no idea how God was going to accomplish it. He works in strange ways sometimes!"

It took the soldiers about fifteen minutes to comb the inside of the factory looking for Ben. The search was widening now to the warehouse and the parking lot. Soon it would encompass the neighborhood.

"Hey nephew! I don't want to be a burden, but it would be nice if we could warp out of here soon."

Elezar composed himself. He was still tired, but he had recovered enough to get them home.

They stood together and he warped the wave. The now familiar sensation took them to the entrance of the colony. They hurried inside. Elezar felt the disruption again as he moved through the entrance. It puzzled him. He wasn't warping the time, but he felt the same sensation.

When they were safely inside Elezar was approached by a very excited Timothy.

"You've got to see this!"

He physically pulled Elezar away from Freddie and Ben. Elezar was exhausted and just wanted to rest but he followed Timothy. They went to the area that held the stored bread. They had an excited, puzzled look in their eyes. Ezra was staring at his chart, tapping it with his pen, counting and recounting the inventoried bread.

"I might have made a mistake," said Ezra.

"No, father you didn't. I carried the bread myself and distributed it!" I know what we had and how much we used!"

Timothy couldn't contain his excitement.

"We used ten loaves at lunch today out of the fifty we had in the storeroom. I took twelve loaves to the meal and when I was bringing back the unused loaves there were fifty loaves in the storeroom not counting the two I returned! I counted them twice."

While they were pondering and recounting, Greta came toward the group.

"The fish, and everything else in the storeroom that we used today, came back to us plus more!"

Elezar remembered the sensation he felt when he passed through the opening a few minutes ago.

"Come with me." He spoke.

The group made their way to the upper floors of the high rise. When the doors to the very upper level opened, a soothing white light baptized them. They were all too stunned to move for a few seconds.

Elezar fell to his knees in praise. The sensation he was feeling at the entrance, the extra food, the soothing light, it all was clear. God was preparing the way. The colony was under His protection now. They were moving into the future ahead of all the troubles the marked would endure. Armageddon was near.

Elezar motioned the awestruck group to follow him. They inspected the gardens. The gardeners on duty were kneeling with a raptured look on their face. They felt the presence of God! They could see the plants grow and expand. The whole area was filling with every kind of fruit tree known to man.

Doors appeared with numbers on them. The group opened one of the doors. The room inside had everything a person needed to live comfortably. Best of all, the same light was inside the rooms.

Elezar led them to the lower banquet hall. He sought out Freddie and Ben to share the good news. His fatigue was gone. He felt the presence and power of God!

I've been doing it all wrong! I've been taking the burden on myself when I warp time. All I needed to do was relax and call on God to guide my way! Elezar thought to himself.

Through the den of the people gathering in the hall, Elezar was alone in his own reality. He felt the gentle shift in the wave and Abe was standing beside him. No one saw but him.

"Well done my son, you have realized a level that few achieve. God does not need us to be burdened with the movement of His time, he wants us to preside over it and let him work. He wants us to be part of his greater purpose and be one with Him!"

Elezar didn't reply. He realized in his stubborn youthful exuberance he had been limiting God, not committing to God. He was never so close to the Creator. It was time to prepare the people for the coming World, HIS Thousand Year Reign!

"You will be required to redeem the one who holds your future. Be unwavering in your Faith!"

Abe disappeared into the wave leaving Elezar puzzled. He didn't understand what Abe meant but he was sure he would know in God's time. Elezar tuned in to the colony, once again part of the present.

13

Revelation

The world was living the Bible's end prophecy. The population of the marked dwindled with each of Egypt's plagues metered out on a worldwide scale. The faithful were in the protection of God and final harvest was at hand.

The red death that permeated the water supplies of the world slowly dissipated, once again leaving water for the masses and for production of the Amy. The marked worshiped their god Satan at the Temple for deliverance. The Deceiver convinced them that their animal sacrifices saved them from Satan's wrath, but the future was uncertain. The only way to ensure their safety was to begin human sacrifices.

The Deceiver and the Beast held a rally broadcast worldwide to proclaim the event. A bride pregnant with a first born would be sought out. She had to be without blemish, an unmarked Jew, and eight months along so the baby would survive the ceremony long enough to die for the Dark lord.

Most embraced the idea. If one or two died to satisfy the lord Satan, especially the unmarked, to spare their lives, then let it begin.

Elezar was in the crowd at the Temple. The Two prophets were preaching even as the broadcast played. It seemed to Elezar that the noon day sun was exceptionally hot that day. He warped out of the crowd and returned to the colony with his news. There were a handful of brides in the compound that fit the criteria, including his own. He had to warn them.

Elezar held a meeting with the Elders to discuss the coming event. It was agreed that he would address the assembly at the evening meal.

The recent changes inside the colony brought so much joy, meals were always a festive occasion. Elezar waited until the end and rose to speak.

"People of God, let me have your attention please. I was doing my daily reconnaissance and learned that any pregnant Jewish woman is in grave danger. DO NOT leave this compound! There has been a bounty placed on you. If they catch you outside of these walls you may be used in their satanic ritual."

"Please, DO NOT leave the safety of these walls!"

He held the hand of his own bride, locking eyes, as he pleaded those words. He knew how hard it was on her to not be on the front lines; not being the catalyst for survival of the colony. He would make it a priority to include her on his missions daily when the risk was very low. He shuddered at the vision of losing her in such a way.

Ben and Elezar were going to make a trip to the bread factory tomorrow to check out the surrounding neighborhood to make sure no unmarked Christian was left behind. It was routine so Elezar invited his bride to go. Her intuition could come in handy on the mission. At least, when she was with him, he knew she was safe.

When the sleep cycle was over, the trio met at the entrance to depart. Elezar whisked them to the familiar confines of the deserted factory. The men left in charge when Ben was rescued tried to make bread with the tainted water. It was so disgusting they were brought before the Beast. In minutes they were all dispatched. No one in the Beast's Kingdom would volunteer to run the factory fearing the same. It was bittersweet for Ben. His factory, his life, was deserted but at least no inferior bread was being produced.

They moved in and out of the surrounding neighborhood under the cloak of the warp. When they neutralized for the sake of investigation, the morning air wafted like opening a furnace door. The sun was so bright the heat waves danced off the roofs and sidewalks like a desert mirage. Freddie became faint. The intense heat sapped her will; her cheeks were bright red.

Ben and Elezar moved her back to the confines of the colony instantly and enlisted the help of the women. A few minutes of cooling wet towel compresses brought her back to normal. She began to cry uncontrollably. Elezar comforted her gently, stroking her hair, kissing her cheek, telling her how beautiful she was to him.

They all gathered to console her.

"Go back to work Elezar! I'll be Ok. I'm surrounded by friends."

She said it, but she wished he'd stay. He was too young and naive to read her body language. The women around her knew. Some of them shook their heads at how insensitive men were. They gathered around her in solidarity. Elezar hesitated.

"GO!" she said.

He and Ben started out again. They got back to the old neighborhood but didn't find anyone. The now noonday sun dried their mouth like the desert winds. They persevered for one more deployment. They came out of the warp close to the Euphrates River. It was already a muddy stream. One more day of this intense sun and it would be completely gone. They returned to the colony.

Elezar spent the rest of the day with Freddie making sure she didn't have any lasting symptoms of the intense heat. Ben and he would go out tomorrow.

Elezar kissed his bride goodbye the next morning and prepared to leave. He could sense her sadness, but it was better she didn't go out in the heat again. He thanked God the light in the compound was steady and comforting, not like the sun.

Freddie lay in bed after he left feeling sorry for herself. There was no comfortable position to lay. She sat for a while in her chair, sitting was a chore, she walked down to the main floor, walking was a limited relief. Her back ached!

To her surprise, Elezar and Ben returned. The sun was too intense to do any kind of reconnaissance. They decided they would go at night, at least the moon would be kinder. She was glad her Elezar was there for her once again.

Freddie was sleeping soundly, exhausted from the responsibility of carrying a nearly full-term infant constantly. Elezar kissed her gently and smiled at the pillow between her legs and the one propping her head, and the one supporting her belly. He wished he could do something for her to ease her misery. He felt so useless around her suffering now. He couldn't fix it!

He quietly made his way to the entrance to meet Ben. They didn't talk. Elezar motioned and Ben followed. They warped to a sector they hadn't checked. In the middle of the night the sun was as bright as noonday. The few hapless souls they saw were hidden in the shade as far out of the sun as they could get, not moving, barely breathing. Their faces reflected the torment of hell. It was too exhausting to even speak. The two time travelers returned to the safety of the compound.

Elezar tiptoed back to bed trying not to wake his bride. She felt the weight shift of the mattress when he lay down. She woke and had to get up to the bathroom once again.

I must have a bladder the size of a pea! She thought as she maneuvered her body through the door. It might take her the rest of the night to get comfortable again!

The intense sun baked the soil that used to be the Euphrates until it resembled broken pottery. Another day and all who bore the heat would die. Ben and Elezar prayed for the wretched survivors. Marked or not they were still God's created beings in great distress.

The duo returned to the colony. They thanked God for His mercy and grace when they retreated to the safety of the compound.

Like a light bulb burned out in a vault, the rogue sun left the world in total darkness. The intense heat had destroyed the electronics in all streetlights. Batteries failed, capacitors exploded, leaving the dark nothingness not known since before creation! The earth gave up its intense heat to the starless sky. Elezar and Ben were helpless. The marked cried in fright for relief from their hell. Elezar and Ben returned home, haunted by the suffering.

The darkness is the Devil's realm. In the confusion, the Deceiver and the Beast managed to breach the secure area around the prophets and silence their voices. They left the bodies in a heap to be discovered when the light of day returned.

The colony was an Eden now. The gardens flourished, the people were well fed and oblivious to the suffering outside their world. Elezar kept them informed and God kept them safe.

The death of the Prophets hit Elezar hard. Along with Ben, Freddie, and Abe, they brought him to the Way. He would be nothing without their guidance. The whole colony mourned the prophets.

The sun returned as if nothing happened, revealing the two deaths. The marked were so relieved to see the sun in its normal cycle and the two prophets gone they rejoiced in the streets. The Realm announced a holiday and declared all should buy each other gifts. Surely now the world would return to normal. The lord Satan had prevailed; the plagues, the suffering was all gone.

14

The Sacrificial Lamb

Freddie knew she should rejoice in her blessings. She had a wonderful husband, a new baby on the way, and a secure life in the compound, but she longed for her old responsibilities. She heard Elezar admonish all the pregnant women to stay inside the compound, especially her. She knew he was thinking of her safety but sometimes he just didn't get it.

She stood at the entrance to the compound reminiscing about some of the missions she and Elezar had been on just to get the bread to the colony. She smiled at the time he almost broke his nose trying to get through the safe house door.

She inched further out the door. The air was charged with the ozone after a rain. She breathed deeply. She couldn't remember the last time it rained! The setting sun painted a beautiful rainbow in the unsettled sky. She couldn't resist. She stepped out of the entrance.

She felt the soft hair against her leg as Rufus, the stray dog that found a forever home in the colony at the insistence of all the children, bolted past her into the freedom of the outdoors.

"Come back here Rufus!" she commanded.

Rufus gave her the look that said "Come and play!" All the time postering and jumping, daring her to give chase.

"Rufus, get back here!" she yelled but the dog jumped in the air playfully and ran a little further.

"Rufus, you get back here right now!" She said with more authority.

The dog decided she wasn't going to play so it turned and trotted away, sniffing and exploring like dogs do.

"If something happens to Rufus the children would be devastated, she thought. The jackals would have him for their evening meal. I'll just go a few blocks and fetch him.

I know this area like the back of my hand, she thought. She cautiously scanned the area for danger. The familiar rush of adrenalin made it seem like old times, but it wasn't old times.

She walked a few blocks when her back began to ache. Her legs were getting heavier with every step. Her hands automatically found their way to her hips, supporting her protruding belly. The discomfort distracted her from her diligence.

Finally, Rufus let her scoop him up in her arms. When she turned to journey back a trooper blocked her way. There were six in all.

Immediately the dog bolted from her arms and started barking. The soldiers kicked at it trying to silence the yapping.

She struggled but was no match for the trained soldiers. She was placed in shackles, blindfolded, loaded into the transport, and whisked away. She overheard them talking.

"She is just what the Dark lord has been looking for!" the leader proclaimed excitedly. "Men, we have just hit the jackpot, we will live out the rest of our lives in luxury!"

This is exactly what Elezar had warned against.

Why couldn't she be content with the blessed life she had. I may never see my Elezar again. Our precious baby may never know his father! All for a disobedient dog!

She began to sob a prayer for forgiveness. She began to sob for deliverance.

One of the men reached over to stroke her hair. He felt the end of the leader's laser rifle stuck in his face.

"You touch her again and you won't live to see the bounty. She has to pass the Master's inspection. If you mark her in any way I'll kill you on the spot, CLEAR!"

"Yes sir!"

The rest of the ride was silent. The transport stopped. The Leader conferred with the guard and the security gate swung open. The vehicle moved a short distance and halted. She felt the shift as the troopers got out. She was helped out of the truck and again surrounded by the troopers. For the sake of her baby, she didn't resist.

She was left in the middle of a large room. She smelled sulfur. Her blindfold was removed. Before her was the one called the Beast, although his name was Nicholas. In the shadows she sensed two beings so evil her skin crawled. In the shadows were the men that brought her in. The last obstacle to their fortune was the approval of the Dark lord. If she didn't pass, they might die along with her. The risk was worth the reward in their mind.

Freddie was approached by two women who forcibly removed her clothes. She stood stripped of all her dignity in the faces of pure evil. She could only close her eyes and try to cover herself with her hands. She felt the evil presence move around her. Although she wasn't touched, she was forced to pose with her arms away from her body. She felt herself lifted into the air and rotated like a sacrificial lamb being checked for flaws. She was placed back on her feet and given her clothing.

They ushered her to a padded cell with a bed and a commode. She got down and prayed for forgiveness. If only she had stayed in the compound. No one knew where she was. Her sorrow was hers alone to bear. She heard the bounty hunters conversing with the Devil.

"I am well pleased with this one. Chione, give these men their bounty and vouchers for the unlimited Amy."

The men were celebrating loudly.

"A million bitcoin!" Frieda heard one say.

So that was the rate for a pregnant Jewish sacrifice! She thought.

She resigned herself to the fact she wasn't going to see Elezar ever again. She wasn't even going to hold her own baby. She wished she had the faith and the gift of time travel like her beloved. She wept.

The women opened her cell door and brought her food. A portion of her uncle's bread was part of the meal. She caressed it, remembering all that it had meant to so many people. She took a nibble.

It was stale.

Her door opened once again, and the two women took away the tray and ushered in two men. They took measurements of her whole body and made imprints of her forearms and hips. They didn't tell her why.

The door closed and she was once more alone in her misery. She reached out her arms and visualized Elezar walking through the door.

• • •

Elezar felt a cold wave all the way to his soul. He shivered as it passed. His intuition told him something was wrong. He couldn't find Freddie. His search got more frantic with every passing minute.

"Has anyone seen Freddie?"

"No, but I'm sure she's around here somewhere," answered Greta in a calm voice.

"Will you help me look?" the frantic Elezar pleaded.

"Of course!" she replied.

Greta enlisted the help of all she met to help in the search. She returned later with a look of concern on her face.

"We can't find her anywhere!" she said, mirroring the concern on Elezar's face.

Elezar and the people in the compound fell to their knees hoping God would reveal to them what had happened to Freddie.

In the middle of the prayer vigil, Seth and his reconnaissance team walked through the entrance. They bowed their heads and stopped in reverence. When the prayer was over, Seth sensed the urgency of the group.

"What's wrong?"

"We can't find Freddie. Did any of you see anything out of the ordinary today?"

"Sorry no, it was a routine day."

He turned to his men and posed the same question. They talked among themselves for a minute.

"It's not out of the ordinary, but there was a transport in the area today with six bounty hunters. They arrived in the afternoon and did their normal sweep of the area. They didn't stay as long as usual and left in a hurry. We were in the other sector and didn't see anything other than that.

Elezar had a sinking feeling. The people touched his arm as he went by offering him strength in solidarity. He made his way to the entrance. He wanted to find clues but there were none. He touched the stone building where he was sure she had stood. He lay his forehead against the cool stone. A memory of the rainbow he saw earlier in the day flashed through his memory. It hadn't rained for so long he stopped to admire the promise of God. He wondered if Freddie saw it too. Tears streamed down his face.

He finally composed himself and turned to go. Seth was waiting patiently for him.

"We don't usually go around the Temple because it is crawling with security but tomorrow, we could go and ask around to see if anyone knows anything." Seth volunteered.

Elezar put his hand on the man's shoulder. He was forming a plan. Finally, he spoke.

"Take a loaf of bread apiece and hide it under your robes. It might be what we need to loosen the tongue of an informant. Meet me here after the sleep cycle. We'll begin fresh."

Seth nodded and left to tell his men. Elezar made his way to their apartment. He lay his hand on the door saying a silent prayer that she would be there when he opened the door. He hesitated, then pushed the door. Even though the space was alive with the soft light, Elezar didn't feel the comfort. Funny thing about God's love. It is given freely but only received voluntarily. Elezar couldn't receive; part of his heart was missing. He slept fitfully.

The sleep cycle finally ended. Elezar struggled to the meeting place, looking like he felt. Seth and his men were waiting. Seth handed Elezar a loaf. They lined single file behind Elezar. In an instant they were in the Temple square. They fanned out in all directions. The morning sun was breaking over the city. The bustle hadn't begun. People were out strolling leisurely past the bodies of the Prophets, sneering at them, or spitting on them. Elezar was drawn to the site. He mourned for them. Only God knows how many Jews they brought to the Way he thought.

He was standing motionless, meditating, thinking of Freddie when he felt a thwack on his shin. He hopped around for a moment, rubbing his leg, looking for the perpetrator.

When he straightened up, he spied a woman who looked to be as old as the city. The fire in her eyes bolted out of wrinkled slits, letting everyone know she was a force to be reckoned with. Her arms and legs gave her the look of a walking corps. A withered hand gripped the equally gnarled walking stick that inflicted his pain. He didn't see the mark on her withered body.

"No, I ain't got the mark, but neither do you." She admonished, pointing the end of her walking stick at his nose.

"Got any food?"

"I might have, if you got what I need to hear."

"I know everything that goes on in these parts."

She put her palm out and motioned with her fingers.

"Food first."

She stood there like a statue. Elezar contemplated for a second.

Even if this old woman doesn't know anything she needs the bread worse than I do.

He reached in his robe and pinched off the end of the loaf and handed it to her. Then he motioned with his hand mimicking her.

"What do I get in return?"

She couldn't reply; the bread filled her mouth.

He waited patiently with his hand out lest she forget her obligation.

In what seemed to Elezar an eternity she answered.

"What is it you need to know?"

"I think my wife was abducted last evening. She just disappeared."

The woman eyed the area of his coat where the bread came from.

"It was last evening about sunset. A transport moved by here and came to a screeching halt in front of the Beast's palace. One guy got out and got through security. He came out a little while later and motioned the rest to follow him. They' a woman bound with a hood over her head in the middle of the men. They rushed her in like she was some sort of high priority prisoner. Shortly after, the men left but she didn't."

She motioned for more bread. Elezar obliged with a bigger piece, showing her, he had more. She savored the bread slowly this time.

"How do I know you're not just making this up?"

She smiled, savored the bread, and took her sweet time answering him. He was getting a little upset. She knew she was getting under his skin.

"You don't now do you? I'll bet you also don't know that she was moved later in the night to another location. I don't know where, but I do know she was surrounded by evil. They's demons around that woman like I've never seen. Before you go all militia and try to rescue her be advised; they are ready for anything. She's not getting' out alive."

Elezar handed her the rest of the bread.

"I know who you are. I know the woman too. You two are legends in my circle. We tell our young about how your people never go hungry because of you and Frieda and that you always have bread! It gives them hope. We'll dole this out, so they all get a taste."

"No, you won't. Come with me."

Elezar led her to the meeting place. When everyone showed He told them what she said. He asked what they found out. Seth conferred with the men.

"Rumor has it she is right. Not as many details but the stories are all similar."

"You men have any bread left?"

They all nodded. They had all of it.

"I want you to follow this woman and give it to the unmarked in her colony. They have had a tough time. God will provide for them too."

Before they departed Elezar prayed, "Dear God please multiply these loaves like Jesus did to feed the multitudes. These are faithful people and deserve your Grace and Compassion."

The old woman had tears in her eyes where the fire had been. She had prayed for so long! The stories that she heard about Elezar were true. He was a great man of God.

Elezar stayed behind. He had to find a way to rescue his bride. He walked in the direction the old woman pointed when she told him they moved Freddie. A few blocks away from the Temple was an unassuming house. Elezar felt the presence of evil around the house. He was formulating a plan. He could warp in the midst and get them both out before Satan's minions could react.

He watched the house for hours. There was no activity. He needed to act soon. His rendezvous with his team was set for an hour. He warped into the house, looking in every place he thought her body would fit. She wasn't there.

He returned to normal. He was puzzled. He saw the women bring her food and leave. Why would they do that if she wasn't there?

These questions flooded his mind. Who created Satan? Where did he dwell until he was banished?

"God. In God's kingdom," he answered the air.

Then he understood. Satan knows God's time also. She was being kept somewhere in time. By himself Elezar could spend eternity trying to be at the same time as Freddie. Only God could make that happen.

Elezar hit his knees in prayer, "Please Lord, guide me, restore my bride to this time so I can free her."

"HAVE FAITH, MY SON. TOMORROW AT SUNSET YOUR BRIDE WILL APPEAR ON THE ROAD TO THE TEMPLE. BRING THE FAITHFUL THAT FOLLOWED YOU TODAY. YOUR FAITH AND OBEDIENCE WILL RESTORE HER TO YOU."

Elezar was relieved and frightened. He would see his bride again, but only if he could be totally obedient to God.

He ran to meet Seth and his men. They gathered to warp home. They had been exposed long enough to the outside world.

Elezar started telling his story to the group as soon as they were home safely. Seth became uneasy when he heard the story. He looked around at his men. They averted their eyes. They wondered if Elezar could have missed the announcement.

"Tomorrow night the first human sacrifice will take place in the Temple," Seth informed Elezar.

To Seth's amazement a calm radiated from Elezar. Not the reaction he would have had it been his bride!

The men sat around the table discussing the mission.

"I forgot in my haste today to get that old woman's name. Can you tell me about her and her people.?"

"Mary, her name is Mary. Her people are dispersed over a wide area with a common meeting place in a series of underground tunnels. That is how they survived. They are near starvation, but our bread will save them for now," Seth said.

Elezar pondered in silence. Somehow, he knew that this event would be epic. He didn't understand the details, but he knew one thing, the woman Mary and her people were involved.

"Tomorrow, Mary's colony must be at the festivities. I feel in my heart that the time is at hand for the final reckoning. Seth, tomorrow I want your men to position the unmarked of her colony behind all the marked in attendance. I'm going to go and warn her."

"If my feeling is right, a cataclysmic event will accompany the sacrifice. Whatever it is, watch the group closely. The ones that bow in worship to God will be brought into our colony. There will be those that run in panic. Let them be. God will separate the wheat from the chaff one more time and we must be ready!"

Elezar pulled Seth aside, "Will you go with me to find Mary and warn her? You know where she and the colony meet."

"Sure, let's go," replied Seth.

The group dispersed. Elezar ate light. He wasn't really hungry but knew he needed strength for the battle tomorrow. He didn't describe it that way to the men, but he felt in his heart that the survival of God's remnant was at stake.

He and Seth slipped into the storeroom and gathered two duffle bags of bread and dried fish to take with them.

Elezar warped the time waves. In an instant they were once again at the Temple. Seth led the way to Mary's colony.

The two entered a dilapidated house blocks from the Temple. Seth went to an interior wall and began moving some pictures hanging on the wall in a sequence only he knew (outside of the colony members).

The wall moved revealing a passage to a tunnel. The two were immediately surrounded by a dozen men armed with the sharpest swords Elezar had ever seen. Their polished surfaces gleamed even in the dim light of the tunnel. One was centimeters from Seth's throat.

"State your business," the owner of the sword hissed.

"We came to talk to Mary; and we brought food," Seth calmly stated.

One from the group came closer to Seth. "He's one of the men that brought the bread. I can still taste that wonderful bread!" he said dreamily. His stomach rumbled.

Everyone heard the involuntary retorts from his belly and laughed.

"We've got more, and some fish to go with it!" exclaimed Seth.

The tension dissipated instantly.

The leader lowered his sword and said, "Follow me."

The entourage moved swiftly through the series of tunnels until they reached a large room. All tunnels reached out like tentacles on an octopus from there.

Elezar spotted Mary sitting on a makeshift chair surrounded by spellbound children. They were enthralled by the stories of how life used to be and the experiences she shared.

She spotted Elezar and Seth and pulled on the top of her cane with both hands until her body broke free of the chair, and she stood upright. She started across the room to meet the two guests.

She wielded her cane like a club when she got close to Elezar and whacked the duffel. "What's ya got in the bag, boy?" she said, the mischief dancing around her.

"You know what's in here, old woman." He shot back.

Elezar knew how to play her game now.

The children gathered around them. Their fear overcome by curiosity.

Mary turned to the children, "Go bring your parents, NOW!"

She struck the floor with her walking stick, and they dispersed.

She turned to the men and admonished them. "Go gather the faithful we have food!"

They trotted off in military style double time, each heading for a separate tunnel.

In minutes the people started streaming in. The room was soon teaming with humanity.

Mary and Elezar talked quietly while the crowd gathered.

"Mary, I have something to tell you about tomorrow. This is something God has laid on my heart and it involves the whole colony."

"I can't believe that God would allow the desecration of his Temple with human sacrifice. I think he will use this occasion to take back the world. We are at the point of the last confrontation."

"I feel He wants me to warn you of some cataclysmic event that is going to happen tomorrow. I need you and your whole colony to be at the Temple celebration tomorrow."

"We never go out in large groups, so we won't draw attention to ourselves. You are asking me to put my whole colony in jeopardy," she replied.

"I know, Mary. I've prayed about this. I've even warped time to try to find out what is going to happen, but I've been blocked. I think God wants me, and you, to take this on faith."

She looked him in the eyes and saw only sincerity. She turned to the crowd and smacked the end of her cane on the floor and then brought it high in the air.

Silence wafted through the crowd. In the stillness she began barking orders to the nearest of the crowd to get a table from the storeroom and some knives to cut the bread and fish.

The people scrambled at her commands. The tables and knives appeared out of the crowd.

Elezar removed his bag and placed it on the table and Seth did the same. They stepped back to allow Mary to speak.

"This is Elezar and his comrade Seth. They have brought us bread and fish that we may survive another day."

A buzz of questions rippled through the crowd.

"Yes, this is the Elezar of the legends that I tell the children. A lot of you thought I was making the stories up but now you can see and taste for yourself.

"Elezar helped his wife Frieda to prosper their colony just like I told you. Now he has brought some of his bounty that we may enjoy God's goodness. Elezar, would you bless the bounty God has provided."

Elezar stepped up to the duffels. He looked out on the gathering. They were sitting on the floor in small groups. Around the table were twelve runners to distribute the food.

He doubted the whole room could be fed on the amount of food they had brought. He placed his hands on the bags and began an earnest prayer.

"Dear God, please multiply this bounty you have provided like Your Son did when he walked among us so many centuries ago. Bless this food as we partake, and may it give us strength for what lies ahead. Amen"

When he removed his hands, they tingled like electricity had flowed through them. He and Seth started removing the bread and fish from the bags as the cutters needed it.

The runners already knew who the very needy were, and they got served first.

As Elezar distributed the bread, tears welled in his eyes. He thought of all the times he stood side by side with Freida distributing the bread for their own colony. He wished she could be here to witness her legacy.

Lost in his own thoughts, he didn't realize what was going on inside of the two duffels. Seth nudged him.

"Hey Elezar, how many loaves have you removed from your bag?"

"I wasn't counting, why?"

Seth replied excitedly, "I've taken a dozen cakes of fish out of my bag and it's as full as when we came!"

Elezar felt his bag of bread and a wide smile lit up his face. He motioned Mary over to witness the miracle. He showed her his bag. She felt the volume for herself.

"Praise God!" She shouted.

She addressed the crowd, "Eat all you want. There is no rationing now in the kingdom of God!"

She danced a jig around her staff shouting Halleluiah. She just couldn't contain her joy and it was contagious. Soon the whole room was shouting and praising God.

Elezar and Seth stayed until every appetite in the building was satisfied. They were filled with the spirit.

"We have to get back. We're going to have a long day tomorrow." Elezar said to Seth. They hugged Mary and slipped back through the tunnel.

Elezar and Seth warped back home. Elezar quietly moved to his apartment. He dreaded another night without Freddie. He steeled himself and opened the door. He felt her presence. He sat on the edge of their bed in silence savoring the moment. He couldn't touch her, but deep in his heart he felt her. Their love transcended the physical. He slept peacefully in the love that God provided. After the miracle he witnessed tonight, he knew tomorrow he would be with his bride.

15

The Ceremony

Satan summoned twelve of his most high priests to perform the ritual. Four men of exactly the same height and weight were recruited to carry the mother of Israel. If he couldn't destroy the chosen of God in the Heavens, he could do it symbolically in his Realm—earth.

By mid-day people started gathering. The atmosphere was festive. The prophets were dead, the rain returned, and the future was set, or so the Deceiver preached. The Human sacrifice would ensure the wrath of Satan was appeased.

He claimed responsibility for all the calamities that befell the earth to give the illusion that he was all-powerful. The Deceiver spun the narrative skillfully; that this was a temporary lull in the suffering, one that could be made permanent and end their suffering if he was appeased by the human sacrifice.

Seth's men came early to position the newly found colony. They were broken into small groups, so they were less conspicuous and dispersed through the crowd. Seth counted almost two thousand in all. The marked crowd was getting larger as the appointed time approached.

Elezar took a position by the entrance of the Temple. He could see the full length of the street. The shadows grew until the appointed time arrived. In the distance Elezar saw the procession approaching slowly. A large gong tolled solemnly in step with the throne.

As she came into view Elezar saw his beauty. Four large men carried her on her throne. Twelve Priests dressed in long flowing robes walked in step surrounding the queen. Gold overlay shackled her forearms but gave the appearance they were part of her. Her legs and feet were covered with braided gold flowing to her ankles hiding her shackles. A tiara on her head held twelve perfect diamonds in a half-moon. Above her head was a single word.

ISRAEL.

The procession was halfway to the Temple when a young man acting like a drunken jester started skipping around the procession trying to impress his friends. They were cheering and jeering him on. The young man lunged at the throne trying to touch the queen.

Without missing a step one of the priests drew his sword and swung it at the man's arm, severing his hand cleanly at the wrist. The procession moved on. The Jester looked on in shock at his stump. The blood was spurting out of his arm at an alarming rate. He picked his hand off the street and tried to put it back.

His friends gathered around, laughing and taunting. They pointed and guffawed when he tried to re-attach his hand.

No one came to his aid.

Too late he realized he needed to stop the blood flow. He discarded his hand like an empty soda bottle and focused on stopping the blood. He squeezed off the flow temporarily, but the insidious red stained his clothing, the street, and his remaining hand. He fell to his knees rocking back and forth until his face turned pale white. His eyes rolled back, and he fell face down in his own blood. His friends moved on, leaving him there to die in the street.

Elezar took advantage of the commotion to position himself in front of the parade. He lowered his hood and looked Freddie in the eye. She saw him and her heart skipped! She knew somehow, he would save her.

He stepped out of the path of the procession and returned his hood. He was trembling. He wanted to storm the men and rescue her now, but he restrained himself. He stood perfectly still, eyes straight ahead. He went into a trance-like prayer. He wanted to be ready when the time was right.

Freddie was carried into the inner sanctuary The four men lowered the Throne and bowed out of the room. One of the priests removed her restraints.

Two more grabbed her wrists and forced her to stand and walk to the waiting alter. She was shackled to the alter on her back.

The Unholy Trinity sat on majestic thrones on the other side of a burning cauldron, unseen by the victim. The ceremony began.

For an hour the chants glorifying the Dark Lord were broadcast on the magnetrons outside the Temple and around the world. The anticipation peaked. The head Priest poised his scalpel to cut the baby out of the womb.

Outside Elezar stood like stone waiting for his cue.

The bloodthirsty crowd chanted yes, Yes, YES!

God's time stood still.

A loud, clear voice rang out, "COME UP HERE!"

The two prophets' bodies rose in a burst of light toward heaven.

Elezar stood like stone.

Frieda's shackles fell to the floor. The priests were thrown into the cauldron amidst screams of agony.

The crowd cowered in fear at the holocaust streaming live worldwide.

The Unholy Trinity escaped to regroup. It was not yet their time.

"REDEEM YOUR BRIDE!"

Only Elezar heard God's command and obeyed instantly!

The curtain moved and he was standing next to Freddie. He lifted her off the alter and carried her to the entrance of the Temple. Elezar put her down on the steps of the Temple and they walked down the steps arm in arm in triumph. When they were out of harm's way the rumble began. The ground beneath them shook.

The image of the beast fell face down and was crushed by the Temple columns as they collapsed. The crowd screamed and ran in all directions trying to escape. A large chasm opened in the earth starting at the Temple and continuing across Jerusalem. Seven thousand marked perished in the earthquake and its aftermath.

When the dust settled the Temple was in ruins. The only people left were Mary's colony and they were on their knees loudly worshiping the Lord God.

Mary shuttered. What if she and her colony had ignored Elezar's warning? The earthquake had just destroyed their catacomb sanctuary!

Elezar helped Freddie to a surviving lawn chair. He motioned Mary over to them.

"Mary, this is my bride, Frieda, Frieda, this is Mary. She was the only one that saw what happened to you. She saved your life!"

Freddie got up and hugged the old woman as much as a very pregnant person can. She felt a tugging in her groin. Water uncontrollably ran down her leg. She grabbed Elezar's hand. Mary saw the expression on her face and saw the wet shoes. Freddie eased back down into the chair.

"This ain't the place for an unmarked woman to have a baby!" Mary said to Elezar while whacking him in the thigh to get his full attention.

"What do you mean?"

She pointed her stick at his nose and then down to the wet spot at Freddie's feet.

"Her water just broke! She's going into labor!"

She swung her scepter at his head to get the point across. He ducked just in time.

"We gotta get her out of here!"

Elezar took control. "Mary, gather your people around us. Do not leave anyone for any reason. We may not be able to come back for them. Make them link hands."

He turned to Seth's men, "Gather the people as close together as possible."

Elezar prayed and lifted his hand. The curtain warped, engulfing the refugees. They were amazed at the peace they felt traveling through God's time. In the time it takes to top a hill at speed and experience the churning stomach, they were standing in front of the colony entrance.

Elezar pushed through the crowd carrying his bride in his arms with Mary following close behind: he was barking orders to the crowd and to Seth.

"Get these people inside as soon as possible. Tell Greta to get them something to eat and get them settled. I need a doctor for Freddie! She's going to have a baby!"

Seth and his men let out a whoop and got started carrying out Elezar's orders.

Greta Saw the old woman following Elezar and ran to her.

"Mary!" she cried.

Greta hugged her and picked the frail bag of bones off the floor and twirled her around. When Mary was safely on her feet Greta started.

"Where have you been? I thought we lost you when we were separated. How have you managed to survive? Who are all of these people?"

"We'll catch up later, right now, Frieda is having her baby. We have to prepare. I'm afraid to leave her alone with Elezar, he may faint at her first contraction!"

A loud Moan came from her room. Elezar rushed out of the room and ran to the women.

"Come quick! Freddie's hurting bad!"

Without waiting for a reply from the women he darted back up to the room. Freddie was no longer in pain. The pain was in Elezar's face!

She started to moan again. She grabbed her belly and breathed deeply. Elezar doubled over in sympathy pain; moaning.

The two women finally walked into the room. The pain on Elezar's face eased when he knew he was no longer alone.

"How far apart are the pains, honey?" Asked Mary, "Bad?"

"I'd guess about five minutes and no, not bad." Freddie replied.

"Not bad! I thought you were dying!" retorted Elezar.

"You've got this Mary, no use both of us babysitting Elezar. I'll go get the new arrivals fed and settled. Send him down to get me when its time." Greta extolled.

Greta grabbed a withered hand and held it next to her cheek for an instant before she left. I was sure good to see her Mentor once again.

Mary busied herself prepping Freddie for birth. Mary put a series of towels beneath her and made sure she was comfortable and got a chair so she could sit at the foot of the bed.

"I'm going to take a peek and see how much you've dilated."

Freddie nodded. Elezar just paced.

"You've got a long way to go, honey. Looks like we're in for a long night."

Freddie started another contraction.

Elezar rolled his eyes, "Isn't there anything you can do, Mary?"

"God and that baby are in control now. Better just relax and savor the miracle of birth."

Elezar paced some more.

"You're driving Freddie and me crazy with your pacing!" Mary said after she had had enough. "Get you a chair and sit down next to your bride so she can squeeze your hand when she has a contraction.

Maybe she'll manage to break a finger, so you'll know a little about the pain she's going through."

Elezar meekly complied. He stayed at her side for hours, laying his head on the bed to rest when she relaxed. The three cat- napped between contractions.

Meanwhile the new colonists were treated to more food than they had seen since the Beast ordered the mark. The guests and the colonists mingled in a festive atmosphere. They milled around getting acquainted, and sometimes re-acquainted, with their hosts. The vigil continued into the night.

Finally, well into the usual sleep cycle, Elezar's world moved. Mary poked him.

"Better go get Greta, It's time."

Elezar raced down to the group yelling for Greta. She was sitting at the end of the serving table reminiscing with some old friends. She smiled, amused at the soon-to-be father's urgency. She got up and excused herself and left. Elezar was off like he was traveling through time. He didn't wait on her.

When she arrived, Mary was instructing the soon-to-be mother on what would come next.

"What can I do?" asked Elezar.

"Stand beside your wife and help her through these hard times!" she instructed for the hundredth time.

She was getting irritated at his whining.

She could see the head now. Greta stood by to assist and cut the cord.

"Ok, honey, we're about done, Give me a good push now!"

Freddie contracted her body with all the strength she had. An involuntary scream echoed through the compound that silenced the crowd. They all prayed silently for this new life born into such harsh times.

There was silence as everyone stood in anticipation.

"Mary cradled the new life supporting its head, pulling gently.

"One more push!"

Freddie panted for a minute and grabbed her thighs and gave every ounce of strength she had. The baby came out.

There was a loud thump on the floor. The leader of the colony, the tough, no nonsense time traveler, had fainted!

Greta laid the infant on its mother's stomach and cleaned out its air ways while Mary tied off the cord and checked the placenta. Right on cue the baby wailed.

"You have a son!" Mary informed.

Freddie smiled weakly. All was well with the world.

Elezar heard the first wail of his new son as he woke to reality. He had a sheepish grin on his face as he stood and regained his composure. Mary's job was done. Greta would stay with the new family for a few hours, but the old woman was exhausted. She found her cane and walked slowly over to Elezar.

He tensed, anticipating a whack somewhere on his person.

Mary reached up and hugged him with tears in her eyes.

"Congratulations, my son. The world renews."

"Sit in this chair," commanded Greta.

She brought his new baby over and placed it in his arms.

"Always support a newborn's head. The neck isn't strong enough yet to hold its head."

She backed away and watched the bond develop that would link father and son for life. It never got old. He rose from his seat and walked, gently rocking his son. Freddie witnessed the moment through exhausted, sleepy eyes. She drifted off.

Greta and Mary left together to get caught up on everything that happened when the purges began, and they got separated.

Elezar sat with his new son in his arms.

Benjamin Elezar Aronivich was going to do great things. He thought, just look at those strong hands and those intelligent eyes.

He laid Benjamin in his crib when a soft knock came on the door. It was Seth.

"I need to speak with you."

Elezar softly closed the door behind him and followed Seth down to the entrance.

"We were preparing to do our daily reconnaissance when we discovered the entrance was completely shut off. We can't leave!"

"The door to the ark has been closed! All the faithful are safe in Eden. The rapture is complete. We will be the honored guests of the Most High God until His Son returns to rule." Elezar exclaimed.

Elezar slapped Seth on the back.

"We've made it! We've made it!"

Elezar was suddenly very tired, ready for a good night's sleep. It had been a very long day.

Of course, little Ben had other ideas!

16

Armageddon

Chione stood in the Command Center of the One World Government. The large monitors all around her each represented a sector of the Realm. Out of the corner of her eye she saw on the nearest monitor the sky light up with a million stars. She looked over the shoulder of the officer in charge of the screen as he zoomed in to investigate.

The magnification revealed that the stars were not stars, but Angelic beings whose garments were pure white. In their hands were weapons like she had never seen. The beings seemed to float on air.

"Activate anti-aircraft lasers!" The officer screamed at his command.

His troops opened fire. Chione watched the laser beams hit the targets but instead of destroying the Angels, the laser energy was absorbed.

Seconds later, after the intense energy was processed, the Angels' weapons erupted like light-ning. The jagged, seemingly random energy struck with such force that every anti-aircraft gun that fired was vaporized. Not one lightning bolt missed its target.

Chione shuddered at the devastation. The officer at the monitor could see the advancement of his enemy glowing translucent white in the night; every detail of the beings unscathed in his first barrage. They were close enough now the soldiers stationed around the territory froze at the sight.

He stood at his station and ordered, "Open fire!"

The monitor glowed white hot with the ensuing carnage. The beings seemed unfazed by the energy thrown at them.

The Angels' slow, deliberate response was like nothing ever seen on earth. The lightning split the atmosphere on its quest to liberate the wicked from their souls. The deafening thunder that ensued announced the gruesome ending to the carnage.

When the battle was over, not a soldier of the Realm was left alive. Their anguished cries as the earth opened and swallowed their souls chilled Chione to the bone.

Her loyalty to Nicholas held steadfast. What else could she do? She burned her bridges many lifetimes ago. Now she must report the latest battle news to him.

She left the war room chaos, got into the hidden self-drive military transport and punched in the pre-arranged code. The vehicle made its way to a secret location known only to her.

She exited the vehicle at the base of a mountain when it slowed for a curve. The vehicle was programmed to keep going so no one could track her. The hidden opening hummed slightly when she activated it with her fingerprints. The door swung open just enough for her to enter and closed with a whoosh. From the outside the door disappeared.

The gyroscopic sphere opened to allow her passage to the catacombs below. Nicholas, once the most powerful man on earth, waited for her update.

The descent gave her time to reflect; *I didn't think it would end like this. Everything I have worked for is crumbling. I was giddy with the power that exuded from Nicholas. Now he hides in the bowels of the earth, waiting for my updates.*

The sphere slowed in the dark tunnel and gently stopped. The door slid open, and she was standing in the dimly lit domicile of The Beast.

A voice she recognized asked, "Did you bring a communicator?"

"No Master," She replied

She knew he was paranoid about being discovered. The communicators were part of the tracking system for the marked. Since she was part of the ruling class, she didn't have the mark so she couldn't be tracked. That made her indispensable to him. A good thing to be, given his history.

"Come closer and give me your report," he commanded

She approached tentatively in the dark silence that was his domain until she could see his silhouette. He was a shell of his former greatness. The drugs had taken a terrible toll on him. The side of his face damaged in the attack was sunken and wrinkled like a corpse. So much so that his glass eye bulged in its socket.

He looks more like his father now she thought.

"The area around the former Jerusalem headquarters has been captured." She began. "Not one soldier of the realm is left there. The sky is filled with beings that possess the power to destroy at will. They seem to use the power of our own weapons against us. Soon they will encompass the earth."

She steeled for his wrath.

He hesitated, reflecting on what she reported.

"Did you know that I've studied all the religious teachings in the world, including the Koran, The Torah, and the Bible."

She puzzled at his response. The last thing she expected from him was melancholy reminiscing about the past. Especially about religion. He continued.

"After the attack I lost a lot of my memory. Except for Revelations, the last chapter of the Bible. It played over and over in my head and the outcome was always the same. We lose Chione, we lose and there is nothing I or my father Satan can do to change that outcome."

"You always thought the drugs were to ease the pain. No, they were to escape reality. I was sent to hell in that attack, but you brought me back to live in predestined purgatory."

She caught a glimpse into his good eye as he paced by. His slip into madness was complete.

"All hail the king of the New World Order! All hail the god of the universe; Nicholas!" His ironic words echoed through the caverns followed by a bone chilling maniacal laugh that seemed to course endlessly through his realm of catacombs.

For the first time in her life, she knew she was doomed. Her choices so many centuries ago tethered her to Nicholas and her dark master. She would spend the rest of eternity surrounded by the evil she helped to perpetrate.

The Sulphur laden air choked her at the realization of her fate. It had never bothered he before. She ran to the sphere.

The ninety second ascent to the surface was eternity. She pounded on the door to release her from her prison when it stopped. The door opened and she tumbled out in terror.

Her knee hit the rocky ground, spurting red. Her hands stopped hard on the surface palms down, embedding jagged rocks in the skin.

When she turned her wrists to inspect them, she saw another set of hands with holes through the wrists but devoid of blood. Her blood filled His palms and ran through the holes in His wrists. She felt the presence of the Savior she rejected. Mercy was gone, Grace was spent. She knew her fate.

Pure terror helped her flee. She ran until her lungs burned and her legs wouldn't move. She bent over panting, covered in spattering's of her own blood. The light pursued her. Over the horizon she saw the flashes and heard the thunder. It rumbled through her body in waves.

She dove under a crevasse in the rocky terrain, evicting the snakes and lizards taking refuge from the storm. Most of them would survive. She would not. From her vantage point she saw a blinding flash hit the mountain.

The ionized air washed the lingering Sulphur out of her nostrils. When her eyes recovered, she saw her master carried into the sky. In an instant his soul was liberated from his useless body and caught up into the swirling hurricane of tormented demons and souls.

She cried for the rocks to fall on her and hide her. The lightening flashed so quickly she couldn't scream. An unseen force separated her earthly remains from her soul and cast it into the swirling melee. The time of reckoning was upon her. Down, down she went into the endless abyss, suffocating from the heat and the stench.

The pure white cloud of destruction moved on, lightening ahead of it and thunder behind. No human was spared God's righteous wrath regardless of rank or position.

17

Satan's Fate

Satan shifted deftly back and forth in the time waves, guiding the missiles, and dodging the wrath of the harvesters. After all, he was at one time the most beautiful angel God created. He knew all of God's ways. Now he used that knowledge to survive.

The Deceiver directed the armies from his command center. He was pacing up and down the aisles.

"I want a report of our remaining ordinance!" he bellowed.

"Twenty-five percent," came the answer from the American sector.

"Thirty-two percent," from the Russian sector.

"Forty-one perc...Uhhh!"

The Chinese commander didn't get to finish his report. His throat tightened with the force of an invisible hand around his neck. His body was lifted off the floor.

A booming voice resonated throughout the compound.

"What are you saving it for?" he screamed.

"You all don't understand! If we don't stop this advance now, we are all doomed. There is no surrender! Do I make myself clear?"

He released his hold on the soldier. The man staggered back to his station.

"I want you all to coordinate your firepower at the leading edge of the advancing light. Create a wall of energy that they can't breech."

The energy was recorded by the thousands of satellites orbiting the earth before they were destroyed by the percussion particle energy unleashed by the battle.

The harvesters stopped to regroup and absorb all the energy thrown at them.

A moment of silence engulfed the compound as the last of the energy was expended. A heavy, hot stench entered the room. The Deceiver bowed instantly.

"We have them on the run. Deploy the nuclear weapons now!" He hissed at the Deceiver.

"Yes, my master." He replied.

As quickly as he had entered, Satan was gone. Shifting, hiding, always moving and stirring evil.

All in the room scrambled to start the protocol to unleash the bombs. The procedure had been passed down through the generations, ever since the bomb's inception in the second world war. Their use had been threatened many times but the total devastation and the radioactive fallout they created, lasting for fifty years, had always been a deterrent; even for the most militant of the people in charge. Until now.

After the Beast threatened to destroy the American province with nuclear power, control of the weapons was consolidated and put under Satan's control. The world was to lead to believe the bombs were being disarmed and destroyed. Only the people in the command center knew the truth.

Every key was in place and every code installed. The red activation button was flashing and beeping to the pounding of every heart in the room.

"Fire the weapons now," the deceiver calmly commanded.

The head of the high command of the New World order walked up to the control and placed his hand on the button and hesitated.

I have done all that the Realm has asked. I have cleared out whole sectors of combatants and enemies of the state. I have destroyed generations of people for the common good but always I thought that I would be part of the New World Order, where people would live and prosper under the Beast. I am a soldier; I must follow orders. The high commander thought, the unrest in his soul boiling. *If I push this button the whole earth will be uninhabitable for the next fifty years!*

This wasn't about destroying to build back better; this was about total destruction of humanity, he mused. He moved his hand away from the button and went for his side arm.

The Deceiver already knew his intentions. The commander flew across the room, hit the wall, and fell unconscious into a heap.

All in the room were paralyzed with fear. The Deceiver pushed the button.

In remote locations all over the world ancient silos opened and burst into flames. The missiles slowly emerged carrying their deadly payloads. Faster, exponentially faster, they flew until their flames disappeared out of sight.

The oceans' surface was broken like a humpback whale's breach, except the missiles disappeared into the sky never to return.

Drone planes carrying death levitated into the fray.

The Creator withdrew his forces. He had provoked Satan to use all his destructive tricks. He always knew that mankind would ultimately destroy itself with the help of Satan.

There was silence over the earth like the calm before a storm.

The first bomb hit. The earth flinched like a bare back under the overlord's whip. Again, and again the overlord's whip flashed until every major city in the world was leveled.

All ordinance was spent. There was nothing left of human beings' tools to inflict destruction.

The wailing and agony rose to the heavens from the ones not immediately vaporized. Their suffering cries echoed in emptiness. They would live in the absence of their Creator for eternity.

Satan shuttered. His strength dissipated like a morning mist as the souls swirled into the abyss. He miscalculated. He thought his strength came from within, that he was equal to his Creator in power. Now he knew. With every soul on earth gone into the abyss he was no more powerful than an angel in heaven.

Anger and humiliation raged red through his scaly body. He scoured the earth to find some souls to enslave, but they were all gone.

On the horizon a pure white vision appeared. Satan rushed toward it until the being surrounded by the light came into focus. Satan froze when he recognized Michael, his brother. They stood facing one another, posturing, moving, positioning for the battle.

"What do you think you are going to do with those chains, brother?" asked Satan.

Michael had golden chains draped around his shoulders that glistened in the light.

"Our Father made them especially for you, brother. They are his special alloy. They represent everything that was evil in your time on earth. A symbol of wealth, and power, and greed. In the New World, gold will be regarded as nothing more than prison chains and pavement!" Michael replied, not taking his focus off his prey.

Michael began twirling the chain toward Satan to distract him. He lunged at him but missed. The battle was on.

Satan warped into a different time followed close by his brother. Michael had learned many battles ago to read the disturbances in the layers of time. Wherever Satan went, Michael was breathing down his neck, toying with him, tormenting him.

They wrestled through time, crashing to earth causing earthquakes and tidal waves. Michael had Satan cornered and partially chained numerous times only to have him slip away. Each time, Michael felt some of the power leave his adversary. It was just a matter of time.

Finally, Michael was able to get the chain around Satan enough to render him helpless. The Angel dragged the destroyer of the world into the present time, where he laid him at Their Father's feet.

"You have served me well Satan. You were the hardest thing I have ever created, for I knew you would create havoc, death and destruction in your wake and appose me at every turn. You used my beloved children as pawns for your evil schemes. And caused untold suffering."

"You see, I created man and woman and gave them the greatest possession any being can possess—freedom to choose. But what good is such a gift if there is no choice? You provided them that choice."

"You helped me winnow the wheat from the chaff. Without you they would have all perished. When I banish you from this world, they face the greatest challenge of all; prosperity."

With that the Supreme Guiding Force of the universe touched the chains, welding them together so there was no chance of escape.

He nodded at Michael, and Satan was banished for a thousand years in the bottomless pit.

18

A Brave New World

The earth was silent, healing from Armageddon. Mountain ranges had crumbled, continents shifted, climates changed.

The touch of the creator eventually calmed the radiated turmoil created by Satan's folly. The Chosen were called from their Edens. The earth was once again ready. The stage was set for the final chapter in humankind's journey.

Seth was on his daily walk. He always walked by the entrance just in case there was a change in the force field. He longed for the adventures and missed the outdoors. He was restless, unsettled, bored.

He was lost in thought, daydreaming of what life would be like in the future. He almost walked by the opening without noticing that the force field and all the stones piled up to camouflage the entrance were gone!

He stepped through the opening unhindered; arms outstretched in disbelief. He stood motionless, scanning the horizon, excitement building. He had to alert the others.

Elezar woke to a pounding on his door.

"You gotta see this Elezar! The force field is gone, and the stones have been rolled away. We can go out the opening again."

Elezar follower Seth to the entrance. They both went outside the compound. Things were different. A lush green foliage covered everything. Buildings were missing. The overpasses were gone. The same light they enjoyed inside the compound seemed to emanate from the sky.

They breathed deep. Of course, they didn't realize it, but the greening of the earth made the oxygen level rise to levels not seen since before the industrial revolution pollution. It was healing.

"I want you to assemble a team and do some reconnaissance. I need to know if the patrols are gone and just what the situation is like before we let everyone go out."

"Ok," Seth replied.

He ran back in the building to recruit his posse. For the first time in a long time, he had a purpose. Elezar went to inform the others, but it was unnecessary. All the doors in the Eden were opened. The people were milling around with a raptured look.

It was time; they all knew the New Kingdom was at hand.

Ben, Frieda and little Ben sought out Elezar. Frieda ran to embrace him. This wasn't a lover's embrace; it was a "celebration of the survival of the human race" embrace, and it was contagious.

Soon every person in the compound was embracing and dancing and praising God.

Only Elezar noticed Seth and his men come back into the compound. Their faces said it all; they glowed with the same light Moses knew in the times of Exodus on the mountain.

"What did you see, Seth?" Elezar asked.

Seth didn't answer right away. He slowly realized he was being asked a question and turned his attention to Elezar.

"All the soldiers are gone! The land is covered with trees and meadows. The roads, all the buildings, anything man-made is gone!"

Elezar collapsed prostrate on the floor. The weight of leadership heavy on his shoulders left from his soul, like the shedding of the bread sacks he carried in the beginning that sustained the colony through the hard times.

The faithful had entered the Kingdom!

He felt a presence in front of him. He felt himself being lifted to his feet. In front of him stood Abe.

"Well done, Elezar," he spoke.

Abe turned toward the opening and began to lead Elezar and the colony out of the compound. Elezar hesitated long enough to put little Ben on his shoulders and take Frieda's hand. It was only fitting that she walked beside him; for without her compassion, tenacity, strength, and abiding love none of them would be where they were.

All in the compound followed like the exodus from Egypt so long ago.

When the last of the people were a safe distance from the parking garage and high rise they called home, the building disappeared; swallowed by the earth with a rumble that shook the ground.

The only way they had was forward. The past was but a bad dream.

Abe seemed to be leading them to the site of the old Temple.

The children chased after butterflies and explored the strange plants growing everywhere. Curious adults caressed the leaves of the unfamiliar plants. Some adventurous souls picked the fruits and tasted them. The atmosphere was festive.

Everyone was so preoccupied with their new surroundings they didn't notice the large male lion that seemed to appear from nowhere to block their path until its' roar shook the air.

Chaos. People ran into each other retrieving wayward children. Children wailed for the safety of their parents. They all gathered behind Elezar and Abe cowering in fear.

What was a lion doing in Jerusalem? Elezar asked himself as he cautiously passed little Ben back to Frieda, not turning his back on the lion.

He stood his ground along with Abe, both ready to move time waves to thwart an attack.

The lion started to close the twenty-meter gap between him and the group.

Elezar hesitated. There was something different about the way this lion behaved and the lions in the wild.

"Abe, look at the eyes," he commanded Abe in a low voice.

"I see it too." He replied.

The lion walked slowly, its head down like a sub-missive dog as it approached.

Elezar held his ground. If he attacks me that will give the others time to flee, he thought to himself but somehow, he knew the lion meant him no harm. Still, he was trembling.

The animal nudged him in the chest, almost knocking Elezar down with his power. The lion then turned and walked away, tossing his head, beckoning Elezar to follow.

Elezar swallowed hard and followed the beast. A short distance away the lion stopped at a tree that Elezar didn't recognize. Elezar stepped back, wide-eyed as the lion's powerful jaws and sharp teeth ripped a large section of the bark from the tree. The lion sat munching on the bark, like a cow chewing its cud.

It nuzzled Elezar toward the tree. Elezar took a strip of the bark and tasted it, then nibbled on it. His eyes got wide when he realized what the animal was showing him. The bark tasted like roast lamb!

Elezar fell to his knees when he finally understood the lion's mission. In Christ's reign there would be no need to shed blood for any reason! The lion would truly lay down with the lamb!

Elezar realized that the lion was gone. It disappeared as mysteriously as it had appeared. He ran back to the group to share his new insight.

The mass of humanity moved on. The curious ran to the tree to taste for themselves. The bark was nearly healed in the short time it took them to reach the tree. One by one, they tasted the tree and brought samples for everyone to share. It was truly a wonderous new world.

The troupe moved on to the place where the Temple used to be. It was a sight never witnessed by humans. A large object the size of a small moon hovered over Jerusalem. The "moon" bordered the former Gaza strip on the south and extended out over what used to be the Mediterranean Sea. It extended almost to the Lebanon border to the north.

Around the large glowing craft was a sea of humanity that seemed to ripple; moving like the glowing waters of a sunset on a serene lake, moving in a surreal, random patterns, bathed in the light provided by the "moon."

The moon-craft glowed with the same light they shared in the Eden. Out of the sky came strange looking aircraft. They resembled stars falling from the sky until they got close to the ground, then they gracefully touched the earth like an eagle.

Elezar noted that the craft stopped long enough for its passengers to deplane and then took off for places unknown, adding more souls to the rippling mass of humanity. His curiosity got the best of him. He walked up to the passengers that just arrived from the closest craft and introduced himself.

"I'm Elezar Aronivich, this is my wife Freida, our son Ben, and my uncle Benjamin Ben-Hadid." He said, looking around for Abe.

The man smiled, still a little overwhelmed by the sight when he walked down the ramp into the New World. He extended his hand.

Elezar took his hand and shook it.

"This is my wife Abby, our sons Duane and James, and our daughter Arlane. I'm David Browning," he said.

An awkward pause ensued. Two strangers who didn't want to be strangers, standing eye to eye but not knowing where to start, overwhelmed by the circumstances.

Elezar finally broke the ice, "I wanted to introduce you to my mentor, Abe, but he disappeared again."

David's eyes got big, "You know Abe?"

"Without him, I wouldn't be standing here," replied Elezar. "He showed me the Way and mentored me through to a Master in God's Kingdom! I still can't believe I'm here. How do you know him?"

"Everyone knows Abe. He traveled between colonies whenever there was a need. He's mentored hundreds."

"I should have known. He didn't stick around in one place for long did he!" Elezar chimed in.

They both laughed. The Joy of Joys (God's presence) filled the air.

"Where did all these aircraft come from?" asked Elezar.

That was the right question asked of the right person. David began telling Elezar about his journey and the origin of the eagles.

"A man by the name of Darious Miller was in the process of developing the craft when I showed up on his doorstep, so to speak. He had the vision, and I had the expertise to make his vision fly. God put us together on an adventure that led us here today," explained David.

How do you get to fly on one of them?" Asked Elezar.

David reached in his pocket and pulled out one of the same silicon-based papers that Elezar touched in his journey to Christ.

"Here, touch this and be patient." He spoke. "An Eagle will be here shortly. We've modified them for the New World. Now, they are self-piloted and will take you where you wish to go by placing your fingerprints on the console control."

"In Christ's reign, we are free to travel anywhere on the planet and enjoy its bounty and beauty any time we wish. We will spend our time on earth learning God's ways and striving to live in His presence, even when the thousand years of peace is past. All of the false gods of wealth and power were banished from us along with Satan in the fiery pit."

"Here's your ride! Enjoy." David ended.

He beamed as Elezar, Frieda, little Ben and Uncle Ben walked up the ramp. It never got old; the humbling fact that his talents were used by God to help in the development of these remarkable birds.

19

Knowledge Is Power

Elezar settled into the control chair. When prompted by the control screen he put on the headset in front of him. He followed the instructions on the screen until a picture of his eye appeared centered in the matrix in the upper corner.

He touched the screen to lock the image into position. The whole ship seemed to open. He had the sensation of sitting in a lawn chair on top of a mountain. He could see in any direction for kilometers.

He put his hand on the orb at the end of the arm rest. The craft seemed to hover in space, no longer tethered to the ground by gravity. He looked up and they were instantly hovering over the New Jerusalem. Wherever he looked the eagle went.

He circled the glowing entity below. It seemed to emanate raw power in the form of the light.

"I counted twelve gates, did you?" he asked Frieda and Ben.

They just nodded, so awestruck by the sights they couldn't speak.

The gates seemed to be fluid, more like force fields that solid gates. As they moved, the gates glowed with the colors and shapes of every precious stone Frieda could think of.

Once in a while, as they moved, the translucent gates revealed glimpses of the interior.

"Ben! Is that gold I see on the streets?!"

"I.. I think so!" he finally answered.

Elezar looked to the heavens. The craft responded. When they were well into space, away from the light, he spoke, "There is no light from the sun and no second-hand light from the moon."

He saw the stars, but they were obscured from the surface of the earth by the only light left. The light of the Son!

Elezar lifted his hand from the orb and the eagle landed in the same spot. David and his family were waiting.

"I was traveling through the waves of God's time, wasn't I?" Elezar asked David.

David replied with a twinkle in his eye. "Yes, I'm surprised that you noticed. Most people don't. That was part of God's update before we entered into the New World. We are all operating on His time now."

"It occurred to me who you were after you left. You're the Elezar that Abe talked about in his lectures. He said that you were his most advanced student and that you were operating right under the nose of the Beast still managed to get all the faithful to the safety of your Eden without the help of the eagles. The proximity to Satan and the Beast and the short distance involved prevented the eagles from being of any help."

"I had a lot of help from people who sacrificed a lot of their lives for the cause," Elezar replied.

As Abe always does, he appeared from nowhere.

"I sense that you have questions. Can I help?"

"Yes!" Elezar piped up, "We have made it to the second coming. Christ is in control. What do we do now?"

"We study, and fast, and pray. Above all, we learn to rely totally on God. There is no need to build houses, or castles, or fortified walls, or accumulate wealth. Everything we need to survive will be provided for us. This is by far the hardest of all trial's humankind has ever endured." Abe explained.

"Although every soul that made it this far is eligible to enter His heavenly kingdom, not all will be able to die completely to self. When Satan is released for the last time, many will follow his false promises to their destruction," Abe continued.

The Group pondered what Abe was telling them.

"Who are the people going in and out of the gates?" asked David.

"Those are the faithful that have completely surrendered, The Martyrs who have gone before, the one hundred forty- four thousand, the prophets; all who have completed their journey and proved worthy for the Kingdom." Abe exulted.

The pilgrimage to the New Jerusalem became a steady flow. They all watched in awe. Time as the world knows was gone. The thousand years was like a day, a day like a thousand years. A peaceful joy glowed from every being brought forth from the new city. The Eagles constantly moved the people to their designated part of the New World.

David, Elezar and their families joined the throng of souls entering the celestial city. No earthly body had ever experienced what they were living first-hand.

All the people known by the scripters that did God's will; The martyrs dressed in the white, the prophets, and the leaders of old, mingled freely with the people. God's Word, manifested in three-D, fill-ing the senses of all the faithful entering and exiting the city!

King Jesus' presence was everywhere at once. When he spoke, everyone heard and listened. His power filled the people until all they could do was shout praises to God.

Truly the New World Order.

Thank You

T hank you for reading ***Armageddon***. If you enjoyed it, please take a moment to leave a re-
view online.

Why I Wrote This Series

Fear. That was my motivation to write this book about end times. I taught an adult Sunday School class and we were about to start Revelations. I studied the last book of the Bible and I was terrified at what I read. This novel is the compilation of my dreams, nightmares, and imagination stemming from that study. I hope it makes my readers think and reflect on the inevitable, and that, after reading this work, you too are terrified about the end times and study the word of God until you can find peace.

Question,

Study,

Believe.

Dan Fulton

About Author

Daniel Fulton lives in Indiana with his wife of fifty years, Suzanne. Together they raised four daughters and are in the process of spoiling three grandchildren. Daniel likes to garden and enjoys sharing his delicious sweet corn every season with neighbors and friends. He has been to Cuba with Living In Faith ministries installing water systems and distributing Bibles to the churches. It has become his passion to get Bibles to the Cuban churches.

In his retirement he likes to write novels and short stories. To enjoy his stories and connect directly with Dan, visit daniellfultonwritingforyou.com.